DARLENE MILANOVICH

by GORDON MARX

 FriesenPress

Suite 300 - 990 Fort St
Victoria, BC, V8V 3K2
Canada

www.friesenpress.com

Copyright © 2016 by Gordon Marx
First Edition — 2016

All rights reserved.

No part of this publication may be reproduced in any form, or by any means, electronic or mechanical, including photocopying, recording, or any information browsing, storage, or retrieval system, without permission in writing from FriesenPress.

ISBN
978-1-4602-8985-3 (Hardcover)
978-1-4602-8984-6 (Paperback)
978-1-4602-8986-0 (eBook)

1. FICTION, CRIME

Distributed to the trade by The Ingram Book Company

DEDICATION

This book is dedicated first of all to my darling wife Gloria, who believed in me from the very first.

ACKNOWLEDGEMENTS

I offer my sincere thanks to all the people
who have helped me with this book.

First, thank you to my friends at
the New West Writer's Group.
Together we went through the manuscript, line by line.

I also want to thank Ellen Edwards for taking
the photo that is on the back cover.

And thank you to everyone else who worked
tirelessly to help produce this book.

Gordon Marx
New Westminster, BC
April 2009

ON NURSES

She goes about in glistening white,
Her cap set lightly on her head;
She smiles and comforts everyone,
Going from bed to bed.

She gives a needle here and there,
Some pills to help them sleep,
Checks each intravenous tube;
Her love for them runs deep.

"Intensive care" is where she works,
Familiar with the pain
That keeps her patients quiet and sad;
She checks each one again.

She usually does a 12-hour shift
Before she leaves the floor.
She's never sorry to be a nurse
But wishes she could do more.

THE ANGELS IN WHITE

It's 2 a.m. in all the land,
A nurse is holding a patient's hand;
The patient, sobbing in his sleep,
Almost causes the nurse to weep.

When the patient quietens down
The nurse continues on her round,
Silently going from bed to bed,
Pondering each case in her head.

Jakes, Emanuel, Godwyn, Gregg,
A lung, two kidneys, a broken leg,
At each bed's end there is a chart;
The nurse knows each of these by heart.

Finished now, she goes again
To try and comfort those in pain;
At 6 or so she has her cup
Then helps those who are waking up.

The day shift comes, welcome relief;
She relays news, both healing and grief.
Now home to bed in broad daylight.
GOD have mercy on our Angels in white.

PROLOGUE

Florence Goldbaum stared silently at the thin writing paper in her hand and smiled. At last, it was all coming together. How many years had she been searching for her father's killer? She could no longer say. But now, victory was within reach.

A bit of research at her local library had finally paid off. Now, she not only had the name of the woman who'd killed her father, but even knew where the murderous witch had fled.

America, someplace called Newark in the state of New Jersey. With a deep sigh, she turned to her small bedroom and began to pack.

Oh yes, she had everything she needed to travel to the United States to continue her search. After all, she had been preparing for this moment for years.

I have the identity; I have the requirements. Haven't I been caring for children now for at least three years? She has children. I will make myself useful to her. I will be her friend. Then, when she least expects it, I will look her in the eye. I will say to her, "I am Florence Goldbaum.

Jacob Goldbaum was my father."

I

Darlene Milanovich got off the plane in Newark, New Jersey on a cold blustery day in March. She huddled against the wind as she made her way to the terminal. The plane had setdown in the middle of the airport because there had been some kind of mechanical problem on board, and the passengers had to walk across the tarmac to get to the buildings.

Darlene was a short husky girl from Siberia, 22 years old, who had just set foot for the first time on American soil. She had short auburn hair barely down to her shoulders and an oval-shaped face, which at the moment was bright pink from the cold, and she spoke acceptable English and cleared Customs without difficulty. Her eyes were bright with the anticipation of adventure in her new home, carefully planned to remove as many pitfalls as possible.

After going through Customs, she had to walk a long way to reach the airport entrance, where she found an information board listing hotels with limo service. She contacted several and chose the cheapest: Darlene had come to the U S with enough of a bankroll to see her through an extensive period if need be, but she wasn't going to pay more than she had to. She called the Biltmore hotel and then waited a half hour before a passenger van with the hotel's name on it showed up. Apparently, she wasn't the only passenger going to that hotel, which was adjacent to the airport.

After registering, she was shown to her room by a young black man who worked as a bellhop: she wasn't used to such service and didn't give him a tip. Throwing her things on the bed until she got organized, she found a telephone book and began combing through it. On hotel stationary she made a list of all the hospitals in the Newark area and then looked up the YWCA. She called to ask if they had rooms for single women, which they did. That would be her next stop. Then she checked the present room noticing the luxurious bathroom and plush bedding. After she had hung up her coat and scarf, she lay on the bed staring at the ceiling and thinking. The long leather boots she wore were on the floor.

After a while, she looked down at her boots and grinned. It had been so simple. She had walked right through Customs without a hitch. Now all she had to do was unload the goods. Sitting up, she took one boot and unzipped it fully. On the inside was an adhesive strip, which she peeled off to reveal twenty perfectly cut diamonds. The other boot had the rest. She plucked each one from the adhesive and put it in a little cardboard box that she had brought for that purpose, then did the same for the second boot. There were forty-two in all, worth one quarter of a million dollars. She stared at them in the box, smiling to herself. The diamonds, nested in a bed of cotton, sparkled in the light from the bedside lamp.

Darlene roused herself from her reverie and closed the box, then taped it shut and tucked it in her purse. She had a decent stash of American bank notes, but the diamonds were her real funds: if she couldn't unload them she'd run out of money in short order. She looked at the list of hospitals and concluded that what she needed was a city map. There were eleven institutions featured on the list, but she had no idea where any of them were.

Darlene was a registered nurse who had worked in hospitals in Siberia and before she came to America. She'd had taken and passed the qualifying exam to work in the U.S. She had also worked as a private nurse, which was where she got the diamonds. One of her clients had been a wealthy diamond merchant and very confiding. Poor man, he should have known better. She wondered if they had discovered him yet.

She smiled again. What a cinch. He was a lonely old man who'd thought that she'd play games with him. She had played along while she got herself organized. Then, when she had her passport, her American money, and a plane ticket, she'd asked him to show her his diamonds again. As he gazed with puffed-up pride at his collection, she'd simply hit him over the head with one of his own lamps and then finished him off. They'd blame it on the thugs that populated the city. Nobody knew anything about the diamonds, he'd told her so himself. She had cleaned out his open safe, locked it up, and carefully removed her fingerprints from every square inch of his house.

When she awoke in the morning, the first thing she did was try out the hotel shower. After some turning and twisting to get the temperature of the water just right, Darlene let the streams of water ease the cramps that the long flight had left in her neck and back muscles. Dressing quickly, she went to find the dining room, where she had breakfast. Sitting in the opulent room, she felt rich but was careful not to look too wealthy. She wanted to blend in and look American. She had been working on her English for years just as if the whole thing had been planned from childhood.

The front desk helped her find a bus that would take her near the YWCA. When she got close to it, she'd get a cab to take her to it. From there she was going to find a job. She couldn't wait to go to work in America. It would make an excellent cover when she began getting rid of the diamonds, which she planned to sell two or so at a time in various pawnshops.

The trip downtown was uneventful and everything went according to plan. She told the clerk at the Y where she was from, and how long she had now been in America. The clerk's eyes widened and she offered to help Darlene get established. Exactly what Darlene wanted to hear.

The clerk told her where she could likely purchase a city map, and she went out of the Y on her first venture. She found the convenience store the clerk had suggested and sure enough, there were maps available. After looking at several, she selected one and bought it. Her first purchase. These would be days to remember, and she savored even the small details.

The Y had a coffee shop open until very late plus a dining room that operated for a couple of hours at each mealtime. Darlene sat in the coffee shop drinking black coffee and marking the locations of the hospitals on her map. The next day she would start filling out employment applications. She smirked as she thought about stating where her "last job" was. But that was all well: she had a good reference from the last hospital she had worked in. The slight snag: the letter was in Russian.

Darlene discreetly surveyed the other occupants of the room, noting how the women were dressed. She had some nice clothes, but she wanted to make sure that she didn't look European. A couple of girls, younger than her, sat not far away, laughing and giggling constantly over something. One wore jeans, a cream knit sweater and a leather jacket. The other wore a similar jacket but had dark slacks and a brightly-colored top.

An older woman sat by herself also wearing slacks and a heavy coat that covered her top. Darlene decided to wear jeans when going to fill out application forms but to wear a skirt and blouse when going for interviews. The older woman appeared to have just come in and looked cold. Darlene grimaced. It wasn't much different from her hometown.

Darlene had grown up in a city called Petronovak. She was the middle child with two brothers. Her father was a mineworker and loved his vodka. Her mother was a housewife who struggled to maintain a happy home. Darlene shuddered when she thought that she might never see any of them again. She loved her family and had left with their blessing. They knew that she wanted something more than to be a nurse in a Siberian hospital.

While Darlene was drinking her coffee, she made trips to the front desk, where the clerk answered her questions. She was amazed to learn the size of the city's largest hospital. The Newark General was twelve stories tall and had six pavilions. This was a must-see.

The next morning she was all set but the weather had taken a turn for the worse. Sleet came down in thick, blinding sheets and the air was bone-chilling cold. Bundled and braced against the elements, Darlene made sure she had all her information, then caught a bus and was soon on her way to Newark General.

It was a big hospital. The taxi rank in front had nine cabs waiting. The main lobby was a madhouse of people rushing about and looking preoccupied or in pain. People on crutches, in wheelchairs, pregnant, pulling IV poles, clutching clipboards, all contending for the same space. Darlene found a vacant seat and sat down enthralled to watch the scene. After a while she sought out the personnel office and asked for an application form.

"What kind of position, honey?" A heavy-set black woman asked in a velvet voice.

"I'm a registered nurse."

"Well we can sure use you around here. Just fill this out and we'll probably call you this week."

"Are there any vacancies?"

Oh yes, honey. There's always vacancies for RNs in this hospital. We jus' eat 'em up roun' here. Do you have your license?" Darlene showed her the forms she had gathered that would allow her to train in the U.S.

"I got some of the forms from the American Embassy in Moscow."

The black lady looked at Darlene and rolled her eyes towards the ceiling. Darlene grinned.

After filling out the application form, she went back out the main entrance and looked skyward. The sleet was still coming down. Instead of catching a bus back to the Y, she had the directions for getting to Willowbrook Center, another hospital.

When she arrived there, she was surprised to see that it was almost as big as Newark General.

She had worked in a three-story hospital that she'd thought large. Willowbrook didn't have as many pavilions, but it was nine stories high in places. She again filled out an application form and was told that there were almost always a number of vacancies for RNs at the hospital. Instead of going to a third hospital, Darlene decided to go back to the Y and wait for a response. She was sure that if the staff hadn't been exaggerating, she'd be working shortly.

At the Y, she changed out of her soaking wet clothes, then got herself a coffee and sat in the coffee shop reading a newspaper. She read about the crimes that had been committed during the previous night and decided that

Newark wasn't that much different from her hometown. She began thinking about her family. Perhaps she should write to them or send a post card. That got her to thinking about money, which led her to reason as to whether or not she should try dumping a diamond or two. She had to open a bank account too, but she wanted to when she had her own place. Thoughts whirled through her head, and she scarcely registered the clerk saying that there was a telephone call for her. "It's Newark General."

She took the phone at the front desk. The hospital wanted to know if she could come in the next day for an interview. Of course she could. She wrote down the time and the room number on her note pad; then she went back to finish her coffee.

The next morning, she had breakfast and then went back to her room to prepare for the interview. It was very important to her to get established in this country and she couldn't wait. She had been talking to the helpful desk clerk about apartments and was ready to move into one the moment she knew where she'd be working. She preferred, if possible, to walk to work every day.

Her appointment was for just before lunchtime. Darlene got there well over an hour early and after finding the correct room, went for a coffee and a donut. This was a new food to her, and while she liked it, she decided not to make this a regular habit. She had to watch her weight anyway and eating donuts regularly wouldn't help.

The interview was conducted by a stern-looking older man who had lost most of his hair. He was wearing a white hospital coat and was shuffling a handful of papers when Darlene walked in, right on time.

"Good morning Miss Milanovich. Please have a seat. I am Doctor Finnigan."

"Thank you." She sat across the desk from him.

"I have your application here. You have a license to work in this country as an RN?"

"Not exactly. I have permission to work as a trainee until such times as I can pass the exams to be a full-fledged nurse in this country."

"You last worked at the Petronovak hospital? How long ago?

"I was working there until two weeks ago. I worked there for five years." She smiled. There were more questions, more paper shuffling, and finally he said that she could start the following Monday on the afternoon shift. She breathed a sigh of relief, thanking him, as she got up to leave.

He had written down what floor she was to start on and the time as well as her supervisor's name. Elated, she now had to locate an apartment that was for rent within reasonable walking distance.

It was still blustery but had turned dry. Darlene went across the street from the hospital and up a side street. It looked to her as if there were apartment buildings on the street and she wanted to make sure. There were apartment buildings along that street and several others, but after an hour of pounding pavement, she hadn't found a single vacancy. Depression began to settle in. She didn't know the city and had no idea where else to look for an apartment.

She was about to give up when a vacant taxi rounded the corner. She hailed it and the driver stopped.

Leaning against the door, she asked through the half-lowered window, "Would you drive me around on some of the nearby streets please? I am trying to find a vacant apartment."

The driver, a swarthy-looking foreign man, nodded. Darlene got in and told him that she wanted to be within walking distance of the hospital. He drove slowly up several streets before she finally saw a vacant sign. As he stopped the taxi, she asked him to wait for her, then jumped out and jogged up to the front entrance, where a sign said that the manager was in unit 202. She rang the unit and a man answered.

"You have an apartment for rent?"

"Lady, I just put the sign up fifteen minutes ago. Yes, it's for rent."

"Can I see it?"

"Sure. I'll be right down." Darlene went to pay the taxi driver, and as she came back, the manager walked into the lobby. He was wearing a torn T-shirt.

"Hi. My name is Al. Do you mind if it's on the third floor? We don't have an elevator." He led the way up to the third floor. Darlene shook her head. He led the way up a set of stairs that was covered in clean brown linoleum, then unlocked the door of a cute but tiny one-bedroom unit. She stepped in, feeling the plush carpet beneath her shoes. A huge window on one side over-looked the neighbor's garden. She fell in love with it.

She was satisfied with the rent and signed a one-year lease. It was Thursday. She had until Monday to furnish it. Walking back to the hospital, she went to the information counter and asked about shopping malls in the area. A large one was within an easy bus ride, and within three hours she had everything she needed, with delivery arranged for the next day. She had the key, so she would stay at the Y just one more night.

The next morning, Darlene had breakfast and then took her belongings to her apartment. Without a stick of furniture, she stretched out on the comfortable carpet to wait, reviewing how she had done so far. Only four days in the country and she had completed her initial objectives. Now she had to be a good nurse to hold her position. Staying employed was important for her while living in this country to keep a low profile and avoid difficult questions.

By ten o'clock, some of her purchases began to arrive. The first was a smart little loveseat that fitted her tiny apartment perfectly. She had bought for the long term, selecting high-quality pieces.

By late afternoon, her apartment was complete except for food. She didn't look forward to this task because she simply had no idea what she should buy.

It was after 7 p.m. when she returned by taxi from the supermarket. She had the driver help her get the bags up to her apartment, then she paid him. He stood waiting. She felt uncomfortable but didn't understand and looked at him inquiringly.

"Where you from, lady?"

"The Soviet Union."

"Figures. Lady, I just lugged them heavy bags up three flights. In this country that calls for a five-buck tip at least!" Darlene stared at him, then dug out a five-dollar bill and handed it to him along with apologetic thanks.

"In this country, lady, everybody always tips the cab driver. Be easy on yourself an' remember that."

Once he'd gone, she began putting the food away, making a mental note that she had to get up to speed on American customs otherwise she would continue to stand out. When she'd emptied the bags, she realized she had bought staples for her kitchen but no salt- or pepper-shakers or utensils as yet. There was a lot more work to do before she had a working apartment, and she sat down to begin making another list.

She did have bed sheets, a pillow, blankets and a radio alarm to wake her up. She still needed a bedside table, which she had forgotten, and table lamps and miscellaneous kitchen items. That would keep her busy the next day. She had noticed that near the mall was a store that bought used goods. She wondered if that included diamonds. Something to find out in the morning.

She made her own breakfast, Cereal, very strong coffee the way she liked it, and a bran muffin. When she was finished, she felt satisfied that she had accomplished something. She walked to the bus stop and waited for a bus that would take her to the mall. It was the one she'd probably catch to and from work, as her apartment was not as close as she would have liked.

The previous day, she had opened an account at a bank branch located in the mall. During the procedure, the clerk asked her if she would like to rent a safety deposit box. On impulse, Darlene said yes and put her little box of diamonds in it. She kept only two with her, tucked safely in her purse.

When she got to the mall she spotted the pawnshop two blocks from the bus stop. She walked back to the store, feeling the nervousness build in her stomach. What would the proprietor say when she showed him the diamonds? The store was called, "Big Bad John's" and advertised that they bought old gold and diamonds. She grimaced. "Well, we'll see".

Skirting around a large wooden barrel, she walked into a store that was littered with the castoffs of many lives. There were radios galore, a glass-topped counter with rings on display; there were telescopes and binoculars and hundreds of other items. Behind another counter was a tall, heavily built man in a necktie and white shirt with the sleeves rolled up. He wore glasses and was doing some paper work.

Darlene went over and stood patiently before him. After a minute, he looked up questioningly. There were other clerks, why didn't she bother them? Read the look on his face.

"Can I help you, lady?" Darlene reached into the small pocket of her purse and pulled out one of the diamonds. He picked it up and looked at her, then reached behind him for a jeweler's magnifying glass and fitted it to his eye, examining the gem carefully. Finally, he put the gem on the counter before him and stared at Darlene.

"Now where would a nice young lady like you get a gem like that?" he purred softly, as if not wanting anyone else in the shop to hear them. Darlene swallowed.

"I brought a few gems with me when I came here from Moscow.

I want to sell it."

"I'm sure you want to sell it, but I can't buy it. I don't have that kind of money on the premises, and the manager handles such purchases as this."

"How much do you think that I could get for it?"

"I'm not sure, but I'd say close to ten grand. Can you come back at four o'clock and ask for Jack Edmonds? He handles stuff like this." Darlene picked up the diamond, thanked him and said she'd be back. She could feel the clerk's eyes on her, as she tried to leave nonchalantly. Back at the mall, she continued buying things for her new apartment, then hired a taxi again to haul a big load of small items home. This driver also helped her get everything upstairs, and this time she gave a five-dollar tip. He took it, looked at it and shoved it in his pocket without a word but seemed satisfied. Darlene felt that she was becoming more Americanized every day. She planned to return to Big Bad John's at four o'clock to see if she could liquidate her first diamond. She thought again about the old man who had paid for the diamonds with his life, and a wave of guilt flooded over her.

Jack Edmonds was fat — at least sixty or seventy inches around at the waist — and could hardly have been more than Darlene's five foot, four inches tall. He wore rimless glasses and knew exactly who she was and what she wanted when she approached him. The clerk had obviously told him about the diamond, but he nevertheless examined it thoroughly and for much longer than the clerk had.

"How many diamonds do you have like this?" he asked in a raspy voice.

"I have several. I brought them with me from Russia to use as capital."

"They aren't stolen?"

"Oh! Gosh! No! They aren't stolen. They were part of my family's wealth." He examined the gem again for several minutes.

"I could give you eight for this. That's eight thousand dollars."

"I thought that it was worth ten," she stammered. He looked at her sharply.

"Are you experienced at selling stones like this? Do you know how much they are worth? What makes you think it's worth ten?" He paused but she simply gazed at him. "I might consider giving you ten apiece if you just tell me how many you have. How about that?"

"I have a few. I will bring you one every month or so until there's none left."

"You won't say exactly how many you have, huh? Interesting… OK, I'll give you ten, but you better keep your word, This is a very fine piece."

Darlene waited while he wrote it up. Then she had to sign two documents. One was apparently for the police in case the gem turned out to be stolen. She tried not to think of the old man's caved-in skull as she scribbled her signature.

Edmonds then gave her ten thousand dollars in various denominations which he counted out and placed in an envelope, watching as she then tucked this into an inside coat pocket.

She walked directly to the bank a block away and deposited all but a little of the money. Now she only had to wait until Monday when she started her new job. She wondered what she should do to kill Saturday night and Sunday. She had noticed a place called a "tavern" in the mall. Naturally she had never been in a bar in America but knew the word tavern. With the money safely in the bank, she decided to celebrate a bit.

The tavern was very dark inside and she had to pause for a few moments until her eyes adjusted. Then she ventured in and took a stool at the bar. Several tables with chairs were scattered around, but she somehow felt safer near the bartender. He was dressed in tight black pants, a white shirt, and a black bow tie. She thought he looked very cute — sandy-haired with a thin moustache and whistling very quietly while he poured drinks for his customers. When he came to her, she muttered, "Beer please" because she didn't know what else to order. When he asked if she wanted any particular brand, she didn't know what to say and shook her head. He brought her a large glass of the amber liquid and she sipped it, then smiled slightly. He nodded and told her it was a dollar seventy-five, which she paid, then added a fifty-cent tip.

The brew tasted delicious. She leaned against the back-rest of the stool, and relaxed, surveying the other customers, checking them over and listening to what they said so that she could learn how to order without standing out. She drank the beer slowly, enjoying it as well as the atmosphere. Music was playing from some machine, country and western songs. The whole thing made her feel good and for the first time since she'd landed, Darlene felt confident that she would make it through.

She realized customers could order food right at the bar, so she asked for a menu and then ordered an open-faced beef sandwich. When it came there was a huge pile of French-fried potatoes alongside. She looked at the plate in amazement and when the bartender slid the ketchup, vinegar and salt down to her, she tucked into the meal, but it was far too much for her, and she left half the French fries. Darlene was weight-conscious and wanted to look slimmer. Her goal all her adult life had been to lose weight, and she decided that now was finally a good time to succeed. However, she had four long slow beers before she left to catch her bus home. Being Russian, she'd built up something of an alcohol tolerance since adolescence. Part of the culture.

Still, when Darlene awoke the next morning her head felt filled with wool. Grimacing, she forced herself to get up, then stumbled around her tiny kitchen, putting together a man-sized breakfast, which she consumed before remembering that she was supposed to be losing weight. She felt depressed. "Oh well, perhaps tomorrow…" After breakfast she went to the corner convenience store for the morning newspaper.

Darlene had deposited virtually all of her American money when she opened her account and now had almost twenty thousand in the bank. She was a saver and had no intention of spending money foolishly. Her parents had taught her how to set money aside and what to save for, and she intended to apply this knowledge in her new home.

She read the newspaper thoroughly and then put it away, thought about the previous evening. In Siberia she had spent time in the local bars drinking beer and was familiar the scene. It was the only outing that she allowed herself back there, and now she was glad that she had done it because she could resume the habit. She was a girl who enjoyed people, music and the atmosphere of a friendly neighborhood pub. What she intended not to do was spend very much money socializing this way.

Monday dawned with bright and unexpected sunshine. Darlene bounced out of bed very early, feeling great and glad that her first workday in America had arrived. Still, she was also a bit apprehensive wondering what nursing would be like in such a large hospital and was worried that she'd have to learn many things over again. She had breakfast and spent the day resting or organizing her apartment. She was supposed to start work at four and end her shift at one am. By the time she left for work she was on pins and needles.

She got to the General twenty minutes early. The seventh floor, where she was supposed to check in, looked jumbled and disorganized with patients on beds in the hallways or wherever else they could find space. "Not much different from Petronovak," thought Darlene. She waited until a nurse seemed between jobs and introduced herself. The nurse said a quick "Hi" and pointed out the supervisor who was sitting at a high counter doing paper work. Darlene went over and politely interrupted her.

"Excuse me, I'm Darlene Milanovich. I'm supposed to start work here today." The nurse looked up and then assessed Darlene over from head to toe. Darlene had gotten herself a nurse's uniform as required and was sharply dressed.

"You're early. You start at four."

"I know but I wanted to give myself some time to get oriented."

"Well OK. I'm Eleanore. Call me Elly because there's another Eleanore on this shift. We call her Lenny. Where did you work last?"

"In Russia. I just got here last week. I have been an RN for five years.'

"You have your license to work in America?" Darlene produced again the sheaf of forms she carried. Elly was looking at Darlene in wonder.

"You just left Russia and you're going to start here today? Boy! You will sure have some adjusting to do. It's not going to be easy, this is a very busy place.

"Hey look girls," she said to some nearby staff. "We've got a Muscovite here right out of Moscow Russia." Four nurses gathered around staring at Darlene and asking her questions. When she told them how long she'd been in the U.S. they said things like, "Wow!" and "That's so brave of you!" and "How has the adjustment been?" When Darlene said she had an apartment on Oak Street, one of the nurses said, "There you go, May, she's got an apartment on Oak. Why don't you get one over there instead of driving all that way?"

May replied haughtily, "I've been trying for three years now. How did you get an apartment over there?" Darlene then related how she'd landed it and they all laughed again. They seemed like a happy bunch. Then Lenny was asked to take Darlene around and show her where things were.

"This is the staff lunch room. You can get coffee here, and there's usually some fruit in the fridge. There's a dining room downstairs where you can get meals." She went on detailing various other locations. Then it was time for Darlene to go to work.

She found out almost immediately that there were no nurse's aides to do the support work. A nurse here was expected to do many things that Darlene had always considered beneath her, which took some getting used to. However, she fit in and was accepted. That was the biggest hurdle.

Days passed. Darlene began to get into the rhythm of the hospital and discover how it functioned. One day she came to the nursing station and saw two police officers standing there. She froze with shock. They were laughing and joking with Wanda, one of her co-workers, but Darlene nearly dropped the charts she was carrying. She stopped and tried to think of where she could go quickly without being obvious, but her mind had simply shut down. She tried to walk calmly to the desk with shivers going up and down her spine, and the cops ignored her.

In Russia, police were very much to be feared and if one saw them, they usually tried to get away and as quickly as possible. Darlene couldn't begin to imagine having a friendly conversation with one of them. On top of that, she was, after all, a fugitive from justice. When the cops left, Darlene tried to sound casual as she asked Wanda what they'd been doing there.

"That tall dark one, he's Frank. I go out with him sometimes," she said, glowing with pleasure from the visit and was obviously proud of the relationship. Darlene then told Wanda how police officers were viewed in Russia. She was still trembling. Wanda told her that in America people thought of cops as friends, but she could see what effect the visit had on Darlene, so she continued talking until Darlene began to calm down.

When Darlene went home the following morning, she sat thinking about the cops while she had coffee. She couldn't imagine not fearing the police, but apparently most people didn't in the US. It was something that she would have to get used to.

2

Darlene soon settled into a routine, working four twelve-hour night shifts each week and taking the other three days off. She had found a large city park with a lagoon and as April began, she spent the balmy spring days walking the trails of the park alone.

As April gave way to May, Darlene was told to get herself a pager if she wanted to be available for overtime work. The hospital remunerated her for some of the costs and being young and strong, she welcomed the extra work, as well as the bigger paychecks. Not all of the nurses wanted to work extra hours, as some had families. But Darlene made herself available as needed: she worked on the day she turned twenty-three and celebrated the following Saturday night by drinking most of a bottle of California wine.

During May, she took two more diamonds to the merchant and put the resulting money in her bank account. One afternoon a clerk for the bank called her and began talking about GICs and other types of long-term investments. This got Darlene's attention and she made an appointment at the bank to discuss ways of getting a higher return on the money that she was storing in her account. As a result she invested most of her savings and was pleased to find that she was able to save a fair bit each month. She also forced herself to eat raw vegetables and avoid sugar. The diet resulted in her gradually beginning to lose weight.

Darlene had hardly ever seen a television set while in Siberia and hadn't bought one when she'd outfitted her apartment. She went for months without TV but found herself wondering when the other nurses discussed interesting programs, so she talked to Wanda and then got herself a nice large set. She began watching a show called, *The Price Is Right*, which she found interesting. Putting it on every morning, she began to imagine herself on stage trying to win something, and when they advertised that one could get tickets for the show, she jotted down the address.

By now she had been fully accepted by the other nurses and given credit for her abilities. She got along well with everyone, and they took turns showing her interesting places in the region. Wanda was single, looking for companionship. Lenny was married with a couple of children, but invited Darlene to her place for supper or lunch occasionally when their shifts permitted it. These outings broadened Darlene's perspective of life in America and helped her become acclimatized.

During July, one of the patients whom she was caring for committed suicide. It was a low point in her career. The person had simply gone to the lavatory, shut the door and was found a short while later, dead from a self-inflicted wound.

On another occasion, one of her patients simply disappeared. He had somehow managed to get his clothes and take off without a doctor's release. Several hours later, he was found at the communal house where he lived. Darlene saw many other things that were new to her as a nurse and heard numerous wild stories that seemed beyond reality, but the teller always swore that the tale was true and Darlene believed, even if she was sceptical.

She sweated through the summer, buying herself new lighter uniforms in an effort to beat the heat. As the autumn came, she watched with misgivings knowing that in no time at all it would be Siberian weather again.

Darlene established communication with her parents as soon as she got her apartment and wrote to her mother twice a month on average. The mail took more than a month to make the round trip. The correspondence was therapy for her because she could tell her mother all her troubles. Darlene had always been her mother's favorite child and Darlene loved her dearly. While her father was often distant, the relationship with her mother had been extremely close. Still, there were many things Darlene wanted to write to her mother about but simply couldn't.

About certain things, she had no one in the whole world she could confide in.

Christmas Day she worked a double shift to avoid staying at home alone. New Years Eve was spent at the local pub where she got kissed by several young men she'd never before laid eyes on in her life. Meanwhile, Wanda had been extending an invitation to Darlene to come on a date with her and Frank. There was another police officer who had noticed Darlene and liked what he saw, but Darlene wasn't yet ready to date a cop.

His name was Mike and Darlene had caught his eye when he'd come in with Frank to visit Wanda. Mike was intrigued by what he referred to as "The Little Muscovite." Wanda kept telling Darlene about her boyfriend and Mike in an encouraging and invitational way, but Darlene held out using excuses of every description but never hinting at the truth. She couldn't imagine herself in the company of a police officer when she had done a man in for his diamonds.

The winter set in with a vengeance after Christmas, and Darlene missed a week's work homebound with a bad cold. It was only after she discovered Buckley's cough medicine that she got over it. There was no such cure in her homeland and she thought it to be the most vile-tasting liquid on the planet, but it did the trick. She enthused about the cough syrup to her friends and acquaintances claiming (with a due sense of exaggeration) that it had saved her life.

When Elly told her that Darlene's vacation period was coming up, she was ready. She had written away to CBS and managed to get a ticket for what was now her favorite game show. She'd had to call Los Angeles to verify that they were indeed taping during her vacation and when her leave time started, she flew out to be in the audience and possibly become a contestant.

Darlene had placed herself in the hands of a travel agent who was supposed to find a budget hotel for her near the CBS studios. But when Darlene arrived at the hotel, she was shocked: it was scarcely more than a huge shack. The desk clerk could hardly speak English, and other Spanish-speaking people were gathered in the front yard basking in the sun. She collected her thoughts and then made her way through them to get inside. The clerk seemed miffed that she intended to stay there, but Darlene didn't know the city at all, and she wasn't prepared to go elsewhere.

Her first night in the hotel was horrible. Loud Latin music played somewhere until almost midnight. Darlene was supposed to get to the studio by 6 a.m. and expected to have had her breakfast before that. Fortunately, she had arrived the previous day and had made a trip to the studio to investigate: it was within walking distance of the hotel. On the way she had discovered several nice 24-hour restaurants and in the morning well before six, she'd had breakfast.

When she got to the studio, about fifty people were ahead of her in line. She fell in behind them and vowed that the next time she'd come even earlier. Everybody had to wait for at least two hours before being processed: they were individually interviewed & given nametags. Darlene began to get excited when they put the nametag on her sweater, because it was exactly like the ones she had seen on TV. After this was finished they were released & told to come back at 11 a.m. for the next part.

She spent the time walking around in the sunshine & having a cup of coffee in a nearby coffee shop. When she returned, her place in line had been determined, and she lined up to be interviewed again by the show's producer. This was when he picked out the ones that would be called to "Come on down!" Each person was given a few seconds to say something about themselves before moving on. Darlene couldn't think of what to say & just mumbled something. Afterwards she regretted not thinking to say that she was from Russia. When the line had entirely moved past the producer the people entered the studio, chattering away excitedly to one another. Those at the head of the line went to the very front and everyone else followed. As she sat down, she saw the stage on which *The Price Is Right* would be filmed. She couldn't believe that she was there-it was just too fabulous!

The MC was standing at the front of the lively and mostly young crowd explaining how and when to applaud. He wanted enthusiasm and made it clear that the audience was to stand up frequently and remain dynamic throughout the show. When they finally closed the doors and the show began, the studio audience went berserk. Everyone was on his or her feet screaming and hollering. The MC was getting everyone clapping, and then suddenly the craziness stopped as the host, Bob Barker, came out. He was a tall, distinguished looking older man who was the epitome of finesse.

Darlene was mesmerized by every aspect of her surroundings. She watched with intent interest, taking it all in and hoping she would remember every last detail later on. She gasped when the "big wheel," an integral part of the show, came into view. It was so small but had looked so large on her TV at home. She was also astounded at how many people were on the stage that one never saw at all on TV.

It was an hour-long show with interruptions where commercials would be put for the television broadcast. During these times, the host answered questions from members of the audience. When the show was over and Darlene was on her way out, she and members of the audience received a card with the date and time that the show would be aired for those who wanted to record it. Darlene didn't have a VCR but was determined to get one when she got back, especially since there was a chance she'd actually appear on TV.

She had every intention of going to all four taping sessions that were scheduled during her vacation period and bee-lined it for the ticket booth. Having secured admission to the other three, she had the rest of the day to herself, so she ambled around the area, shopping in a few stores and making an effort to become acquainted with at least this area of Los Angeles.

The next morning she was at CBS earlier but by no means early enough to be at the head of the line. She grinned to herself. These people were diehards: they must have gotten here at five o'clock in the morning, maybe even earlier, when she was just getting up. Still, she was quite near the front of the line, which satisfied her. After yesterday's experience, she was familiar with the procedure and hadn't yet had breakfast, knowing there would be time for that after she had been processed.

Everything went just as before and the crowd was even livelier though that scarcely seemed possible. Lots of young people were hollering and screaming out cheers while they waited in line. Darlene, who was essentially quite conservative, found the whole scene mind- boggling when she thought back to her hometown. She couldn't even begin to imagine such excitement taking place in Petronovak.

This time when she stepped in front of the producer she managed to blurt out that she was from Russia but living in New Jersey. This information seemed to heighten the producer's interest, and he asked her a couple of questions before she moved on. In the studio she managed to get a seat right near the front. She realized that this location would get her on TV when the cameras scanned the audience. She made up her mind that aside from buying a VCR to tape the shows when she got home she would also send a copy of the tape to her mother. Her mother didn't have a TV let alone a VCR but there was probably one in the community that she could use.

During this second show she still wasn't called to be a contestant, and although she knew that only a handful of people in each audience was selected, she still was disappointed and could hardly wait for the third show, which was being taped the same day in the afternoon. The result was the same. Although Darlene was enjoying herself immensely, she wanted to cap her vacation by being a contestant on the show, not just a member of the audience. This was, of course, entirely in the hands of the producer.

The next morning she was there even earlier, but there were still about twenty people ahead of her in line. She didn't mind and even made friends with the people standing directly behind her, an older couple from Montana who told Darlene all about life on a ranch.

Although in a cheerful mood, Darlene knew that this was her last chance of being told to "Come on down!" on *The Price Is Right*. Tomorrow she was flying back to New Jersey. She probably would never do such a trip again. It was now or never. The producer seemed indifferent to her as she stepped up & gave a short spiel about herself. Everything went as usual, right up until just after the first spinning of the wheel. There was the commercial break, and then as if through a fog, Darlene heard her name being called! She couldn't believe it and turned to the older lady from Montana.

"Did they say Darlene Milanovich?" she asked over the din. The woman looked at her, grinned and screamed, "Get on *up* there!" Darlene struggled to her feet and into the aisle. Hands grabbed at her to wish her luck and a dozen people mobbed her as she scrambled to the front.

She had been called to "Come on down!" at last!

Suddenly she was extremely nervous. Not fully recalling how she had reached the stage, she stared up at the host, who was looking down at her with an elegant grin if such a thing were possible. As if to make her more welcome, he silenced the audience and then said in a velvety voice, "Welcome to *The Price Is Right*, Darlene. Could you please tell the audience what country you were born in?"

"Russia." yelled Darlene into her microphone and the crowd roared again. Then the show began in earnest. A dishwasher was brought out for the contestants to bid on, and Darlene won the bid. Now she had won a dishwasher! Next, she climbed up on the stage and positioned herself beside Bob. He then made more out of the fact that she was from Russia by asking her how long she had been watching the show and whether or not it was available in her homeland. She obediently answered his questions and found her nervousness disappearing.

The host did often enjoy teasing his contestants and now, he started in about how she'd like to win money, lots of money. Darlene smiled a bit timidly but remained silent. As the doors to the prize opened, it became clear that she was going to play Plinko; the audience was being whipped into a frenzy. Darlene had never seen this particular game, but she heard the host say that she could win fifty thousand dollars.

In a daze, she did as she was told, won herself four disks, was given a free one for a total of five, and then sent up the stairs to play the game. She looked down over the board and put one of the disks on it. It began sliding down through the pegs and she won five hundred dollars. She put another on the board and it went into the zero slot. With the third one she won ten thousand dollars! She couldn't help giggling.

The host asked her if she was enjoying herself and when she said yes, prompted her to play the fourth disk. She won another five hundred dollars and with the fifth disk hit the zero slot again.

Darlene was exhilarated beyond her wildest dreams. Would she ever have a letter to write to her mother now! She got to spin the big wheel but was beat out for the showcase showdown. Still, she had won eleven thousand dollars on *The Price Is Right*!

The next morning, Darlene got up early and loaded her luggage onto a bus that would take her to the airport. She had filled out some forms and been told that she'd receive her winnings in three to six weeks.

She had written down the dates that the show would likely air and, of course, was now definitely going to tape it at home. Ironically, she could hardly wait to get away from the sunny climes of southern California and back to the chilly weather of New Jersey, where she could tell everybody about her experience.

When Darlene returned to work from her vacation and told the other nurses what she had done they were ecstatic. She decided that on the day the show aired, she would have a party and invite the other nurses to come to her apartment to watch. Elly, Wanda and Lenny all said that they'd show up and when the day came, they watched Darlene as she was called down. They laughed and cried as she went through the game. Darlene taped the show as did Lenny and Wanda on their own sets. It was one of the highlights of Darlene's life.

One day while Darlene was on shift, Frank and Mike dropped in while they were on duty to see Wanda. The other woman was at that moment very busy with a patient, so Darlene tried to make small talk with the men until Wanda was finished. It soon became clear that Wanda wasn't going to finish very soon and since it was time for Darlene's break anyway, she ended up going down to the dining room with the two cops. She still felt nervous about police officers but she'd seen these two around so many times and taken so much ribbing from them that she was beginning to relax in their company.

Mike paid for her supper, which was a nice gesture even though the meal wasn't expensive. She sat chatting with the two uniformed police officers noticing the envious stares that she was getting from other nurses. By the end of the half-hour break she'd agreed to go out on a date with Mike providing that they went out with Wanda and Frank. Mike felt pleased that he was finally going to go out with the cute little Muscovite. By the time they went back upstairs, Wanda was just finishing up. She heard about the planned date and enthusiastically agreed to double-date with them. The cops then went back to work, their lunchtime mission accomplished. Darlene, on the other hand, went home that night wondering what she had gotten herself into. Never in her wildest dreams had she thought she would date a police officer!

Darlene had plenty of time to fret about her decision since they could only do it when both Wanda and Darlene had the same evening off. In the meantime, Wanda chattered every afternoon about Frank and what a nice guy he was. She said that they usually went to the "Red Dragon", a nice cosmopolitan restaurant and dance hall. Apparently, there was usually live music there and both Frank and Mike loved to dance. Darlene, on the other hand, had never set foot on a dance floor.

Two weeks went by during which time the guys had checked back to see when they were going to go out but were told that the new shifts hadn't yet been confirmed.

When the next shifts finally had been posted, the two nurses didn't share a single night off. So they'd either have to wait even longer, or one of them would have to take a night off without pay. Either one of them would have to phone in sick or with some other plausible excuse, but neither one of them wanted to jeopardize their positions at the hospital. Elly knew what they were planning and if one called in sick, she'd be very suspicious.

Meanwhile, Darlene had been conscientious about unloading her diamonds regularly. She now had a healthy bank account plus some GICs in which she'd invested. Scattered among the apartment buildings where she lived were a few small houses that had escaped the wrecking crew. One, a three-bedroom bungalow right next door to her building was put on the market. Darlene saw the "for sale" sign one day and wondered how much they were asking. As luck would have it, she saw the owner was in the yard working, so she asked him. "I have it priced at around two fifty, but it's best if your real estate agent talks to mine. Then we can still be friends while they fight it out." He laughed and Darlene smilingly agreed: she had never spoken to him before, but she got the message.

While visiting the mall a few days later, she noticed a realtor's office and ventured in. After explaining what she wanted, she was quickly turned over to one of the realtors who said that she'd get right on it and asked what kind of an offer Darlene wished to make. They discussed options and at last agreed that the saleslady would figure out a lower but still reasonable offer for the house.

That afternoon before she went to work, Darlene got a call from the agent saying that she had submitted an offer on Darlene's behalf and that the next step was the owner's. By the end of Darlene's shift the following morning, the agent had come back with a counter offer that Darlene had to think about for a while. In the meantime, she received a thorough tour of the house and arranged to have it professionally inspected. She was becoming acquainted with something entirely new and was rapidly getting used to the idea of owning a piece of property.

In general, it was a buyer's market. Darlene's realtor bargained until she got a price that she was comfortable with. The deal went through although it still took nearly three months before the house was empty, and she took possession. She had paid all but fifty thousand of the price in cash, which made getting her mortgage much easier. During this time, she and Wanda had finally gone out on the date with Frank and Mike, and Darlene found Mike to be good company. They had laughed and joked around the whole evening and had even had two consecutive double dates since.

Mike was quite surprised that she was in the middle of a real estate deal, and his estimation of her rose. Although she spoke almost perfect English there was an occasional slip when she would reveal her thick Russian accent. She'd blush and correct herself, but there was no question about it that she was Russian. Mike found the little Muscovite to be "cute" and "nice to be around." She was getting to enjoy being around him also. In fact, he was with her when she first entered the little brown house as her own property. It was empty and clean but she knew that it would need some fixing up if it was to suit her.

When she next saw May, one of the nurses at work, Darlene asked her if she was still looking for a place closer to the hospital. When May said that she was but didn't have time to go house hunting, Darlene suggested that they have the evening meal together. Over their bland but passable dinners, she talked to May about renting Darlene's house, either on her own or to share with other nurses who also wanted to live adjacent to the hospital. May was definitely interested and agreed to come for a look at the house the next day. After a tour, she was excited about renting the place and sealed the deal with Darlene. Now, she would canvas the hospital looking for a couple of other nurses to share the costs. Guaranteed there would be no shortage of candidates because many of the nurses wanted to live in the area but couldn't find accommodation.

Darlene happily helped May get the house ready to accommodate other tenants. Darlene was finding that she enjoyed dabbling in the real estate market, so she made plans to do this some more. When she discussed her ventures with Mike, he was dumbfounded. Here he had thought that she was just a little nurse from the backwoods of Russia when in fact she was acting and talking more like a tycoon.

Darlene invited Mike up for an after dinner glass of wine one night and as they sat talking on her love seat, he suddenly slipped his arm around her and kissed her hungrily. Surprised and swept off her feet, Darlene found herself responding with her own kiss, and it was some time before they broke off. She stared into his large soulful eyes and sighed. He was what she had been missing, and she didn't feel lonely anymore. Eventually, Mike left but he knew that it wouldn't be long before the kisses led to other things. He decided that he'd do whatever was needed to go to the next level.

Darlene tossed restlessly that night, but sleep didn't come. She was in love.

At 2 a.m. she gave up on sleep and got up to write a letter to her mother. She was certain that she would never agree to go to bed with anyone without the benefit of marriage, and she wasn't sure that she wanted to take that step. However, she knew that she couldn't just say "no" to Mike. He had to be given some consideration also. She didn't finish the letter that night but by the time the sun was sending its first rays above the horizon, she decided that if Mike was interested in talking marriage, she would at least hear him out.

3

Mike and his pal Frank were partners when they went out from the station to combat crime, and they also enjoyed leisure activities together. Both were outdoorsmen intocamping, hunting, and fishing. Mike, in fact, owned a lodge on Lake Pinto a few miles from Newark. He kept the place fully stocked all the time and had built it so that one could fish off the back porch. The two men were young and ambitious but good-natured about everything.

Mike was now actively pursuing Darlene with the intention of becoming her lover. After a lengthy conversation with her a few weeks back, he was becoming used to the idea that the only way he was going to get her into bed was to marry her. Darlene had remained rock-steady on that point.

On their next stretch of shared days off, the two couples headed out of town to Mike's lakefront property. The lodge had two large bedrooms, one used by the women and the other by the men. Beer flowed freely and there was lots of good food. There was also a canoe. It was Sunday morning, and Mike now had Darlene near the centre of the lake in the canoe. He drew the paddle out of the water, slipped it under their seats and sat motionless. Darlene looked at him questioningly. He then smiled lopsidedly and reached in his pocket to take out a small box, which he passed to her. She reached forward and, still leaning towards him, lifted back the lid. The large diamond of an engagement ring glittered in the sun. She gasped, in delight and then in wonder.

"Well?" said Mike, a huge grin now spread across his face. "Well what?" Darlene would wait until he said the words.

"Will you take my hand in marriage?" Mike said almost mischievously. Darlene squealed and nearly capsized the canoe trying to reach Mike so that she could kiss him. After some awkward climbing, they sat in one end of the canoe laughing and kissing, while the other end of the canoe lifted out of the water.

They drifted along the lake in the sunshine for most of the afternoon discussing wedding details and future plans. Mike wanted to get married almost immediately, while Darlene wondered how she could ever arrange for her family to meet him. It was a significant stumbling block.

When they finally came in off the lake, Wanda and Frank had a delicious meal of freshly caught trout waiting for them. Mike and Darlene were tanned from the sun and glowing with happiness leading Wanda to remark that the fresh air seemed to have had an especially positive effect on them. They both laughed and exchanged quick, knowing glances.

"Do you have anything to tell us?" queried Wanda hopefully. She knew full well that Mike was getting desperate and would do almost anything to achieve his objective and wondered what they had been doing out there so long. Mike winked at her, and the truth came spilling out. Frank poured some champagne that "just happened to be" in the lodge, and they toasted the newly engaged couple. Then they wanted to get in on the marriage plans and the evening was spent in deep discussion of numerous possibilities.

Darlene had, of course, finished the letter to her mother some time ago. Indeed, she and her mother were now in fast and furious communication as she prepared for the happy day. Darlene desperately wanted to have her parents at the wedding, but that could only occur if she sent them plane tickets to travel from Moscow to the U S. and then back. She and Mike discussed this at length and agreed to postpone the marriage until her mother and father could be there. At least two months was needed to secure passports and visas, so the wedding was set for three months from the date of their engagement. Darlene realized that she would also have plenty to do during that time.

4

The house that Darlene had purchased was now occupied by May and two other nurses who had been searching for accommodation adjacent to the hospital. May had taken thehouse at a fixed rent and then sub-let the two extra bedrooms. One night the three nurses were having what started out to be a quiet party. Somehow a few young men later managed to crash the party and when asked to leave they became loud and irritating. Although trying their best, the nurses were unable to control the situation and the men ended up on the lawn, where they proceeded to wake up the neighbors. Someone phoned the police — and guess who showed up.

"Isn't that Darlene's house?" Mike looked on in astonishment at the large gathering on the lawn. Frank nodded.

"Do you think that I should go wake her up?" Mike asked somewhat taken aback.

Frank didn't think so and the two cops got out of their car to break up the party. Several young men ended up in handcuffs on the ground, and one of these fled wearing the handcuffs. He was later captured and found to be wanted on a serious criminal charge. May was mortified. She also thought about waking Darlene but decided against it. Darlene instead found out the next morning when Mike came around, making an "official call" to inform her of the night's events.

She couldn't understand how such a mess could have happened but said that she would, of course, cooperate fully with the police. Darlene waved good-bye to Mike, then turned to the phone; she was furious at May and intended to lay down the law about wild parties. However, once May got a chance to explain, Darlene accepted her story, and they discussed how to prevent such intrusions in the future. Afterwards she ended up giggling about what had transpired during the night, and the fact that her soon-to-be husband had been called in to break up the party. At the same time, she speculated about what Mike would think of her if he ever found out the truth about her.

It was bad enough that she had bopped somebody over the head and stolen a fortune in diamonds from him. Even aside from that, she didn't know what Mike would think if he ever found out her true net worth (but not how she had achieved it). At present Darlene had about four hundred thousand dollars socked away in investments and the number wasn't going down. In fact, it had been increasing steadily over the past few years, and she spent time monitoring the markets to ensure her financial situation continued to improve.

After spending quite a bit of time at Mike's lodge on the lake she had started to think about getting something like that for herself before realizing that pretty soon things wouldn't be just for her alone, and she wouldn't need her own lodge if she was married to Mike.

Relinquishing such sole financial control was a huge step for Darlene. She had to remind herself daily that one day soon she would no longer be captain of her own ship. That aside from money, she would also have to share her bathroom with a husband. It made her so nervous at times that she could hardly function. "How am I going to make this marriage work?" ran continuously through her mind.

One thing she did was organize her financial situation so that it would require no attention for at least a year. That would give Mike time to adjust to the idea that she was relatively well off. She had no idea as yet how she was ever going to explain this to him, but she definitely couldn't fabricate any explanation that would involve her parents — they knew nothing of their daughter's wealth either.

Very soon after Darlene had emigrated, her mother had written that "a man who lived in the city had been killed by thugs". She thought that Darlene had worked for this man occasionally but wasn't sure. Darlene nearly flipped out when she read the letter and wondered if any one else had made that connection, but since then, nothing else had surfaced.

The diamonds had been liquidated eons ago and she now had all the money invested. Some was placed in five-year or one-year debentures, and all was tucked away out of sight. In addition, working as a nurse meant her income comfortably exceeded her relatively modest monthly expenses.

Time flew by. At last the day arrived to meet the plane that bore her father and mother from Russia. The meeting was a dazzling display of three people who hadn't seen each other for several years. Her mother engulfed her in a bear hug. Her father stood to the side waiting to give his daughter an affectionate kiss on the cheek. Then Darlene then escorted them to a mid-range hotel where she had reserved a particularly nice room, and then she stayed with them as long as she could before going to work. The next day she'd bring them to her apartment where they would meet her husband-to-be.

5

After learning of Darlene and Mike's engagement, Frank wanted to hold a stag party for Mike and began to make plans. Initially, this seemed fine to Darlene, but when she found out(through Wanda) that there would be strippers and lots of booze, she put her foot down. If he didn't think any more of her than that, she'd reconsider marrying him. Mike was initially astounded at her attitude but fairly swiftly relented, admitting that going to a party with lap dances and such didn't show much discretion on his part. Instead Frank and a few other cops took Mike to a bar, where they attempted to get him stinking drunk. He avoided that pitfall as well but had a good time nevertheless.

May was the nurse who was responsible for the party that had gotten out of hand. She was an older nurse but still enjoyed a good time. The party had been her idea and afterwards, rumors about it circulated around the hospital. May got ribbed by lots of nurses and even some doctors for the "orgy" that had taken place at her house.

She managed to laugh at all the rumors, but her house had become known as the current place for a good party. As a result, May was coerced into holding more parties on a frequent basis. However, none ever got out of hand again.

She found that for a relatively small fee she could hire a security guard who would make sure that no one came to the party who wasn't invited. Then, to offset this expense, May collected a donation from all the attendees during the party. As a result, there was at least one party every week at May's house, and almost everyone who attended worked at the hospital. Doctors began coming to the parties with their wives. The parties were clean with good music and lots of fun. Frank and Mike even dropped in occasionally to check up on things and were impressed. May's reputation grew and she became popular at the hospital.

Darlene was now just one week away from becoming a bride but wanted to call the whole thing off. She was so nervous that it hampered her ability to function as a nurse. People congratulated or joked with her about the upcoming wedding, but she was losing sleep.

Only her mother managed to give her strength. Mrs. Milanovich had not been at all impressed with the idea of her marrying a police officer until she met Mike. Then she was all for it and encouraged Darlene as much as she could; during the week before the big day, she spent practically all her free time at the apartment.

Darlene had managed to get her weight down and was a trim one hundred and twelve pounds on her five-foot-one inch frame. Her hair had been done by a top-notch stylist and the wedding gown made her look angelic. She was as ready as she'd ever be.

Mike showed up in a tuxedo. Frank was his best man, while Darlene had three of her closest colleagues as bridesmaids. The wedding took place in a Russian Orthodox church in the heart of the city, with a hundred guests, give or take. Mr. Milanovich gave the bride away and the bride cried buckets during the ceremony. The reception went on until 4 a.m. by which time Darlene and Mike were already long gone to prepare themselves for a week in Barbados. Darlene had never been to the Caribbean and was very excited. She and Mike had both been granted vacation time even though technically, the deadline for applying had already passed. Elly had appeared reluctant to give Darlene the time off and reminded her that such a special privilege happened only once in a lifetime, then smiled broadly and wished them the very best. Ironically, Elly herself had to take time off to attend the wedding.

When Darlene returned to work, she had a gorgeous suntan. She was a married woman and reluctantly gave notice to her landlord. Then she and Mike went looking for an apartment that would be large enough for them both. Both Darlene and Mike worked afternoons, so they had the earlier part of each day to conduct their search. Eventually they found an apartment that met their requirements. Then Darlene had the job of managing the furniture disposal. There were two sets of furniture between them, neither of which could be retained: everything had to be replaced by bigger and better-quality furniture.

Darlene's mother had been very impressed with the U.S. Her father had spent some time looking around and he also liked what he saw. They went back to Petronovak with the intention of extracting themselves from their situation there and then emigrating to the States. Darlene was happy to hear this but also had misgivings. Her father was a mine-worker. What would he do in the U.S.? She had a hunch that they wouldn't mind living off their daughter's income, but she had no intention of letting that happen. Another hitch was that, her father and mother didn't speak English as well as she did. They could be understood, but their accent was obvious. Darlene had worked hard to perfect her English. She had hardly any accent.

As Mike and Darlene set up housekeeping, Darlene tried to get used to what her husband did for a living. He carried a gun and had a dangerous job. He didn't take unnecessary risks or do anything unprofessional, but every workday carried the potential of injury or death. She found this to be an unanticipated source of stress. He seldom talked about his work, just as she didn't talk about hers. However, sometimes she read about his activities in the next day's paper, and then she'd get nervous or upset. She told herself that she didn't get married to a man to have him shot up at work.

They were at Mike's lodge every time they could get away from work. There was no landline at the lodge but Mike had to bring along his pager and mobile phone. Darlene also brought hers, but they were less likely to be used. The two of them would sit on the back porch fishing, kissing, hugging, and talking about the future. Mike told her that he'd like to buy a hobby farm someplace near the mountains. With some gentle probing, Darlene got him to open up about it and describe his vision. When he was finished telling her what he wanted she murmured that she had the money if he could find the property. He laughed and told her it might cost a lot naming a rather substantial figure. She smiled and said that she could handle that.

Mike could tell that she was serious which prompted him to ask her just what kind of money she had lying around. She was slow to answer, then remained vague about it. This started a serious discussion about matters financial, which Darlene lost. Mike came to the conclusion that he had married a nurse who was fairly well off. He let it stand at that but decided that he liked Darlene more every passing day.

One day Mike took Darlene to a sporting goods store. At least it looked like a sporting goods store but it had a shooting range in the basement. First he showed Darlene an assortment of guns. Then he made some suggestions as to which one she should pick out for herself. She couldn't believe that he was trying to get her to buy a gun. She had never thought about it until she got married, but now she felt that she hated guns. Nevertheless, at his insistence she picked pout a snub-nosed .38 that looked cute — it was so compact. Mike purchased the gun, and then they descended to the range, where he said he was going to teach her how to shoot it.

Darlene had thought that buying the gun was the end of it, but now, she was learning to shoot! She wanted to back out but couldn't, so she put on earmuffs and let him walk her through loading and unloading the gun. Then he got her to load it. When she did so, he told her to shoot at a target some distance away. When she missed the target, he showed her what she'd done wrong. This went on for hours. By the time they left the range she could hit the target consistently, and Mike was impressed by her swift progress.

Mike had every intention of taking care of his little Muscovite, but now he didn't have to encourage her to co-operate; she was intrigued by the gun and wanted to become an expert marksman. Darlene went to the firing range almost daily to practice, and her ability to shoot increased steadily. Carrying the gun to and from work was different though. She wasn't particularly interested in having the weapon with her all the time. However, Mike was adamant and she relented. Darlene got herself a purse and began carrying the firearm everywhere. Then to her surprise and consternation she discovered that not only Wanda but many other nurses carried a weapon as well. She began to love the gun she carried and considered it an important part of her wardrobe.

Darlene had her gun properly registered and thus had a permit to carry it, but she knew that getting it out of her purse in an emergency would be almost impossible. She discussed this with Mike, and they fitted her with a holster that she could wear under a sweater or jacket. It was easily concealed — small but deadly. If she had to carry it at all, she felt much safer having the gun easily within reach.

Whenever they went to the lodge now, she and Mike would spend some of the time at target practice using cans in the yard. Eventually she became almost as good a shot as Mike, who was compelled to keep in practice.

Darlene had gone along with Mike on the gun issue. However, she found it difficult to reconcile the woman she used to be with the one she now was. The gun still frightened her in a way, but she didn't share these thoughts with Mike.

Even before she met Mike, Darlene had occasionally experienced fear while going home from work. Once a drunk had stopped where she was waiting for the bus and tried to grab her. She easily knocked him off his feet because he was already nearly unconscious from liquor, then she helped him back up as she apologized and watched him stagger off. She had often thought about how vulnerable she would be if someone really tried to attack her. But she didn't feel vulnerable anymore.

6

Darlene and Mike were the talk of the town during their first year of marriage. Wanda & Frank often joined them at the lake to spend the weekend but now the two women didn'tshare a bedroom. Wanda slept with Frank without the benefit of marriage. Darlene disproved but said nothing. Mike and Darlene had discussed their future and how children would fit into it. Neither of them wanted children right away and both of them thought that their careers were far more important than setting aside time for child rearing.

Darlene carried her gun automatically to the point that she was never without it. She had written to her mother about carrying a weapon and her mother was aghast. She couldn't understand at all why her daughter felt it necessary to have that kind of protection.

On a few occasions, Darlene had encountered what looked like trouble on her way from or to work. She often asked herself what she would do if someone attacked her. She couldn't see herself killing somebody again but then, it might be different if it actually came to that.

One afternoon as she came out of her apartment, two young men were waiting for her. They had been stalking her, finding out her routine and wanted to capture her for their own pleasure. She had no idea that they were after her until their large black sedan pulled up alongside her on the street. She immediately noticed that the street was deserted except for her and the sedan. They were career criminals who were afraid of nothing and fully intended to do with Darlene as they wished.

The car stopped right beside her. One of the young toughs jumped out to grab Darlene. He almost got her into the car before she shot him in the stomach. The gun was pressed tightly against the man's flesh and made only a muffled report but the driver, realizing what had happened, stepped on the gas pedal forcing the car forward in a lurch that threw Darlene to the floor of the car. The guy she had shot was left bleeding out onto the sidewalk. She struggled to sit up and then putting her gun to the driver's head, ordered him to stop the car. He did so then she then shot him dead.

She got out of the car and went on to catch her bus to work. On the bus she sat where no one could watch her while she reloaded her gun. She hadn't left any fingerprints in the car, she was sure of that because she was wearing gloves. Both the punks were dead, she was sure of that too. She forced herself to act calmly while at work and gave no hint that she had just finished killing two people. Later she wondered why she had the ability to remain calm under such circumstances, and why she could kill with impunity and without remorse.

The following morning she left work and went by bus directly to the lodge, then took the canoe out to the middle of the lake and disposed of the one thing that could tie her to the two shootings. She got back home by mid-afternoon and paged her husband to tell him that she had "lost" her little gun. When he asked where she'd lost it, she said that it was at the bottom of the lake. He arranged to see her at the hospital and came when she was about to take a break for the evening meal. They sat off in a corner where no one could overhear their conversation.

"Your gun is in the lake? How did it get there?" he was calm, but his eyes were narrowed in concentration.

"I was canoeing this morning. Last night was bad and I needed the solitude. I dropped it in the lake accidentally."

"You have to file a report about it, and I guess we'll have to get you another." He refrained from lecturing her on safe habits or responsibility. They then talked awhile longer before both had to return to work. He had never before heard of her rushing up to the lake to go canoeing, and he had a small but nagging sense of worry. When he found out about the two punks that had been killed near her place, he became even more worried.

In fact he was fuming. He was sure that her gun was the weapon that had killed the two, but he had absolutely no proof. She hadn't said anything to indicate this and had appeared perfectly calm. He could scarcely believe that she'd lie to him about something so important, and yet two men were dead and her gun was at the bottom of the lake.

The following morning he picked her up at work, and they went out for breakfast. He observed her guardedly but could find nothing to indicate that she had recently murdered anyone. She was her normal, calm, cheerful self. Mike began to think that he had made a mistake.

When he casually mentioned that the bodies of two men, dead of gunshots had been found in the neighborhood, she didn't so much as blink an eye, and Mike felt almost certain that she didn't know anything about the incident. He proceeded to tell her all about the shootings and then all about the men. They were criminals who preyed on young women; they also dealt in drugs and stolen property. Mike had dealt with them on a couple of occasions, and in his view they were sociopaths. Killing was too good for them On the other hand, from the law's point of view, whoever had killed them was wanted for questioning. He watched her as he spoke, but Darlene showed interest only to the degree that any wife would show when her husband was talking about something.

After a long breakfast they went to the sporting goods store where she picked out another gun that was almost a duplicate of the one she'd dumped in the lake. Mike supplied her with a form for reporting her lost gun, which she filled out and left with him. He'd make sure it got filed when he returned to work. At last, they both went home and collapsed exhausted to spend the rest of the day in bed. That night, Darlene walked along the sidewalk beside where she had murdered the driver of the car. She didn't feel any remorse.

Sitting in the cruiser the next day, Mike realized that he hadn't asked his wife why she'd had a bad night before she went up to the lake. The night in question was the one when the two men had been murdered so he once more couldn't make up his mind. He was a police officer but also a husband. Should he trust his wife completely or should he act like a cop? He couldn't make up his mind.

7

While Darlene and Mike worked the same shift, Mike was often at work more than Darlene because he put in more overtime. He was often required to appear in court or be available to appear. Besides that, if a call came through near the end of his shift, and he had to investigate an incident, he just stayed on the job until he'd done as much as he could. There were times when, by the time he got home, Darlene was ready to start the next day's work, and several days might go by before they saw much of each other again.

After the double killing, this set-up was welcome to Darlene, as she didn't want Mike around asking more questions about how she'd managed to lose her gun, or why she'd gone the lake by herself. She realized this point was especially curious because she knew better than to go out in a canoe on the lake with no one else around, and Mike knew that she knew better.

From her husband's point of view, Darlene's presence there was still very sketchy. Even though they had been married a year, Mike wondered just how well he knew his wife.

She seemed so cool sometimes when he would have expected her to react emotionally. She also seemed so capable of handling stress. Part of that might come from being a nurse, but he wondered just how she would react under other sorts of pressure. Despite the danger of doing so, he talked with Frank about his concerns. Frank placated him and told him that he probably had nothing to worry about. Frank knew Darlene quite well and couldn't imagine that she had what it took to kill two people and then carry on as if nothing had happened. By the time they'd talked it through, Mike felt that he was over-reacting.

From then on, he tried to show nothing but love and adoration when he was alone with Darlene. He succeeded, and she seldom thought that he was being a cop around her. When he did ask her too many questions she'd laugh and say, "Is that Mike the cop talking or Mike the husband now?" Mike would blush and ease off.

He therefore never did find out why she'd had a bad night that night, and conversations about her work became few and far between. On the other hand, she quizzed him regularly about his work now, claiming she was concerned about his safety.

8

Darlene had always had a passport, but when they went on the honeymoon, she'd had to have hers re-issued in the name of Darlene Strong. She was after all, the wife of MichaelStrong. One day when it was getting close to Darlene's vacation time, Mike asked her if they should go visit her mother and father. Upon their return, he told Frank that had he known, he would have sooner taken a short trip through hell.

Darlene was astounded that Mike wanted to visit Russia. She started to tell him about the numerous problems they would face but then thought that she might be paranoid. Nevertheless, she told him about general conditions over there and tried to dissuade him from continuing his line of thinking, but Mike had practically made up his mind. The last thing that Darlene wanted to do was set foot in the Soviet Union again, but she could never tell Mike why. A long, almost heated discussion ensued over the next few days with the upshot being that Darlene and Mike Strong were going to visit Petronovak for two weeks.

Darlene had allowed herself to be convinced that Russia was more civilized than when she'd left and that going there was perfectly safe. During the days after the decision was made, she was on automatic at work with nothing on her mind but how she could get out of going back to Russia. She thought of every plausible excuse and cast each one aside. The more she protested, the more suspicious her husband might get. She could only hope that any danger to her from the Russian police would now be minimal. Darlene also wrote to her mother, a long entreating letter, begging for understanding and help in this dilemma. Her mother was overjoyed that her daughter and son-in-law were coming to visit, which didn't help matters in the least; but she also quietly applied for and received exit visas that she would hold for them "just in case".

Vacation time came all too swiftly for Darlene. Mike, on the other hand, was looking forward to the adventure: it couldn't come soon enough for him. In Newark, they boarded a plane that would take them to New York, where they would transfer to a plane for Moscow. In Moscow they would catch an overnight bus that would take them eventually to Petronovak. It was called an "overnighter," but they would actually be on the bus for three days. However, it was the most feasible way to get there, and Mike could have his fill of the Russian countryside during the trip.

Everything went according to plan. Darlene led the way, and Mike followed. She seemed to know her way around, getting them into the country easily and on the correct bus. After that she spent most of her time resting or pretending to while she worried herself almost sick over what she was getting into.

The bus trip was uneventful. They traveled, ate, slept and traveled until Darlene hoped she'd never see another bloody bus in her life. She was in a foul mood by the end of the journey, but seeing her parents waiting at the bus terminal cheered her up. They again hugged and greeted each other like long lost relatives and then walked the forty blocks to her parents' home.

They walked rather than pay the $150 U.S. the taxi driver quoted them, and because they had been sitting for almost three days on the bus, and also because it was a nice warm but not too sunny day. Mike couldn't get enough of the sights around him as he walked. He took dozens of photos to show Frank and Wanda.

The Milanovich house was small but had been fixed up so that there was a place for everyone to sleep even if the partition was only a curtain. They intended to stay for one week. The first thing they all did upon arrival was gather around to have tea and black bread, which Mrs. Milanovich had made. She was all smiles and jokes as she put it on the table. Mike couldn't understand why Darlene would rather be anywhere else on earth than in her mother's kitchen. He wondered whether something was going on with his wife that he hadn't been told about.

But his concern was temporarily buried beneath the pleasure of all these new experiences.

During the first two days in Petronovak, Mike and Darlene went on walking tours of the city. She took him to the hospital where she used to work, among other places. Mike was interested in having a conversation with a Russian police officer, but Darlene did her best to distract him. She persistently pulled him away whenever they spotted the police and lied as best she could that they weren't actually police but rather soldiers who did police work. She made it clear that she was terrified of them and that he should be too.

"They aren't like police officers in the U.S., Dear." she said flatly as if that was the end of the subject. But it wasn't. One day Mike was on his own and managed to engage one in conversation. The first thing that the officer asked him was if Mike was registered in the district. Naturally he wasn't and made light of it. The officer unsmilingly told him to bring his passport to the station that day or face either expulsion or imprisonment. When Mike got back to the house he asked Darlene why they hadn't registered at the police station when they came to the district and she knew that he had been talking to a police officer. She turned white with fear and then red with anger. Running from the room she threw herself on the bed and sobbed.

When Mike came in to talk to her she slowly calmed down and told him of the letter she had received from her mother about the murder that had taken place during the time that Darlene was leaving the country. She said that if the police felt like it they could throw a person in jail without charges, and it'd be months before she or he found out what was going on. They could stay locked up forever, and no one would help them get out. She also explained to Mike the disadvantage of being so far from Moscow, where they otherwise could get help from an embassy. Then she asked Mike to recount exactly what the officer had said to him and she listened carefully while she tried to think of what they would do.

9

Darlene didn't have to go to the station to register because that afternoon the police came knocking at the door of the Milanovich house. Mrs. Milanovich answered the door andspoke to the two officers in Russian. Darlene heard her say that her daughter and her son-in-law were visiting from America. The officers pushed their way in and demanded to know why the couple hadn't registered as visitors to the district. They demanded all documentation, and Darlene envisioned her passport being deeply buried in some government file while she waited months to be processed. Her face was a mask but she was scared stiff.

In the end they didn't take the passports and visas, but told both Mike and Darlene that they were to come to the police station the next day to register and be fined for not having done so before. They said it would be just a small fine, a formality. When they left, Darlene immediately began packing her belongings and told Mike that they had better clear out while they still could. Mike still didn't see the problem and Darlene screamed at him,

"They want to investigate me for a murder. Now let's go! She was crying and babbling as she tried to explain it. Mike's face was granite. Now he knew why she hadn't wanted to come here in the first place. He had no idea whether or not she was involved in a murder, but clearly she was scared of being questioned about one. "Maybe" he thought, "she's afraid of being questioned about a couple more, too."

There was a quick family conference. Darlene wanted to scram, and Mike wanted to register at the station. Both of Darlene's parents stated that if everyone didn't get away that night they could all face persecution and worse. Mike couldn't believe it, but Darlene's mother shot out the door and was gone. She hadn't said where she was going but returned with a man who was willing to lend them a tiny German car to flee in. Mike began to get the idea that they were serious. They would leave the car with the man's sister in Moscow and had better get right on a plane. That's what the man said, and Mike quivered with both fear and anger.

The car barely held the four of them with a small amount of luggage for Darlene's parents plus their own cases. Mike remembered how far it was to Moscow by bus and thought of what it would be like in that car. He decided that he'd do the driving. What he hadn't been able to figure out was why Darlene's parents had to come. When he brought this up, it was made clear to him that they'd be charged with, among other things, harboring fugitives and would never see the light of day again. He accepted that. By now he was willing to go along with them, as they seemed to know what their police were like. He remembered the look on Darlene's face the first time she'd seen him. Now he was beginning to understand.

Mike drove and Darlene initially sat beside him. After a short while, though, she asked Mike to pull over so that her father could sit there while she took the cramped rear seat. Mike found out that Darlene didn't know how to drive, which astounded him. During the journey, he got to know her father even though the man had a heavy accent, which made his English hard to understand. Mr. Milanovich knew how to drive because of his mine work, so he took the wheel for a while. It was a hellish trip. They were continuously afraid of being stopped by soldiers. After several hours, Mike found a roadhouse where they all slept round the clock, and then they set off again.

They pushed the little car to the limit and made it to Moscow in two days. Darlene helped direct them to the residence where they were to leave the car. After that it really was one hundred and fifty dollars to get to the airport by taxi. During the ride, Mrs. Milanovich revealed that she had exit visas for herself and her husband.

"You have visas? How come?" Darlene was both thrilled and puzzled. How could her mother have known that they would be fleeing the country? Whatever the explanation, the news was a tremendous relief because getting her parents out would have been tenuous without the visas. Now it was a lot more likely that they might make it.

They found rooms near the airport and rested while waiting to depart. Their tickets were made out for the next day and rather than arouse suspicion by changing the departure date, they decided to wait and try to look casual as they left.

When they checked in at the airport counter there were soldiers everywhere. Darlene didn't refer to them as police anymore, just "soldiers," telling Mike that the distinction was faint, at best. She also told him to relax- there were always dozens of soldiers at the airport checking everybody in and out. Darlene was sure that being this close to leaving they'd make it. She only hoped that the northern police hadn't yet spread word to Moscow of their being wanted.

At last, they were on the plane. It was an American airline that had landing rights in Moscow. Darlene crossed her fingers and sat tensely in the seat. She couldn't wait to see the plane moving to the runway. Finally it began taxiing out across the tarmac to the runway, and after a brief wait they were accelerating, then airborne. They were on their way!

When the plane had reached altitude and leveled off, the captain came into the seating area. This was highly irregular behavior, and Darlene began to feel edgy as she watched him have a brief discussion with a stewardess. He then turned and came directly to Mike and Darlene. Mr. and Mrs. Milanovich were sitting several rows further back and watched the scene anxiously.

"Are you Mr. and Mrs. Strong?" the captain asked, bending forward and speaking in a low voice.

"Yes." It was Mike who answered. "Your parents are named Milanovich?"

"Yes." Darlene's voice was barely a whisper.

"The control tower radioed for me to turn back and land. They urgently wanted to take you all off the plane. As you can see, I ignored them but if you're wanted for something, I have to notify the police in the States. They may arrest you and send you back to Russia, or they may not."

Darlene and Mike looked at each other. She had tears in her eyes. Mike looked grim. They told the captain that they'd be happy to talk to the police stateside. "In fact" Mike said, "there's an American cop on this plane," and he showed his badge. The captain thanked them for their co-operation and returned to the cockpit.

When they finally got back to New York, there were indeed FBI agents waiting to escort them through Customs and into a little room off to the side. They all sat down while the agents examined their documents. Then each one was asked in turn to tell their story while one of the agents took notes. When they had all spoken, the agents allowed them to continue the journey to Newark.

In the wee hours of the morning Mike and Darlene arrived at their own apartment after having dropped off her parents at a motel. They stumbled into bed thoroughly exhausted, and just before they turned the lights out, Darlene, trying to sound light-hearted, asked, "Well, honey, where would you like to go on vacation next year?" Mike didn't make an immediate reply. Now, more than ever, he was certain that his darling little wife had something to hide. How was he ever going to find out what that was?

They had planned to come back with a few days of their vacation left in case they needed to rest up. Now, they slept from midnight to noon before rising to deal with Darlene's parents. The four of them immediately began searching for an apartment for the Milanoviches and found one before Mike and Darlene had to return to work.

They had received a clean bill of health from the FBI and had no worries there. They had to stock the apartment with absolutely everything and wondered how long they would have to continue spending before the Milanoviches had some kind of income.

Darlene came up with the idea that her parents could apply for refugee status. It seemed a reasonable plan since to remain in Russia would have meant incarceration or worse. She worked her shift and then went to a government agency to start the process. Then she went to visit her parents to let them know what she was doing. It also occurred to her that buying the hobby farm would be a good idea. When she and Mike were next talking together she broached the subject and asked him if he could find a suitable country place for her parents. He told her about a couple of places that seemed interesting, and they drove out in Mike's car a few days later to look at one of them.

It was ten acres, mostly wooded with a creek. Darlene fell in love with the place and decided that she would buy it with or without Mike's permission. Mike had wanted a place for him and his wife not for her parents. Darlene explained to him that they could build another dwelling for themselves on the property but she needed some place to put her parents.

Even with what had happened so far, Mike was still smitten by Darlene and could deny her nothing. In fact, the longer he knew her the deeper he fell in love with her. Anything she wanted she got — he couldn't resist her. So they drove back to town and went to the real estate office where they sealed the deal. Mike was still apprehensive about Darlene's ability to put up the down payment, but she came through with half the total price, which shocked Mike and re- awakened the thoughts that sometimes troubled him.

With the paperwork done, they simply had to wait for the place to be vacated. Then they had to clean it up to their satisfaction before the move. Her mother and father had been told about the new place and looked forward to it because they were having difficulty adjusting to the American way of life. They were to be caretakers of the property, which Darlene and Mike would develop to suit themselves. They intended to go skiing both with skis and with snowmobiles on their property. They also planned to acquire a couple of horses which the parents would look after. There was a whole pile of new kinds of activities in their future.

Wanda and Frank were invited to be part of the hobby farm right from the start and were consulted about what kind of residence to build that all four of them could use. They also suggested a skating rink, an idea which Darlene liked because she was an excellent skater.

There was already an outdoor shooting range where Darlene would be taught how to handle a rifle. Mike was also determined that Darlene was going to get herself a driver's license.

The house on the hobby farm still needed quite a bit of fixing up before it was entirely suitable for Darlene's parents, but the neighboring farm had what looked like scarcely more than a shack. It was very run down and obviously in a state of neglect. However, when Mike and Darlene spent time on their place they couldn't help but notice the amount of activity and visitors at the other place. Various vehicles were coming and going at all hours of the day and night and it didn't take long for Mike to become curious and inquisitive. He talked about the situation with Darlene but he didn't stop there. When he was at work he filed a report about the place, which started an investigation.

The next time he was at their farm, he noticed an undercover police officer staking out the next-door place. Mike only noticed because he knew the man. Then, one day a couple of weeks later, Mike recognized one of the cars and subsequently one of the visitors. He was a drug dealer and well known to the police department. This time when Mike made out a report, he was told to curtail his activities on his own hobby farm and not be seen anywhere around there until the investigation was further along. The hobby farm was in Darlene's name since she had made the down payment and was responsible for the mortgage. She and Mike decided to contract out the rest of the repairs to a well-known and reputable man who promised that he would make the place the way they wanted it.

Both Mike and Darlene were concerned about her parents' safety if they began living on the property, so the Milanoviches had to wait for the investigation to end. It did at last, but not before some drug dealers had a shooting war on the property, which brought out the police in large numbers. Numerous people were arrested and two got killed by other criminals. The shack was burned to the ground in an attempt to hide the evidence of a major grow-op.

Thankfully, the contractor was unfazed by all the excitement and even completed the work slightly ahead of schedule. With the restoration of the house finished, Darlene at last moved her parents onto the property at last. They loved it on sight and settled in easily. After several interviews with immigration officials, the U.S. government had accepted them as refugees from Russia and were even paying Mr. Milanovich a small monthly sum, which made them feel that they were somewhat self-supporting. Darlene still had to help them out financially but was helped out on the farm. While Darlene referred to her dad as "father," his real name was Fred. Her mother's name was Dolly, but again, Darlene had too much respect for her mother to use that name and called her Mum. Shortly after the Milanoviches moved on to the farm, the contractor and his team started the new large residence that would be used by Darlene, Mike and their friends. Then the horses and the snowmobiles came. It was springtime, there was hardly any snow left, and the house wouldn't be ready until well into the summer, but there was going to be one big celebration.

The property next door had been up for sale since shortly after the shootout. It was also ten acres and had some out-buildings on it but nothing else. When Darlene heard the rock-bottom price she couldn't resist: the owner was apparently terrified that it would somehow continue to be a hang-out for criminals, and he wanted to be relieved of it. So Darlene added it to her collection and now had a hobby farm of twenty acres. Mike just watched in awe. He had admitted to himself long ago that he couldn't begin to keep up with his little Muscovite.

When Darlene got her driver's license, there was nothing that could stand in the way of her getting a car. She told Mike that she was in the market for a vehicle if he wanted to help her choose, but when they began talking about it, it was obvious that she already knew what she wanted. The job was to find it. Darlene had always envied those who drove a Mercedes. In Russia, it was the car of choice for the upper crust; the soldiers all drove them as did government officials. She wanted one but didn't care if it wasn't new. Mike took on the task of searching one out and eventually found her a vintage sports model that met all her requirements. He told her about it and carefully watched her face as he quoted the asking price. Naturally she didn't blink, and he wondered if he'd ever find out just how much money she had.

They went one day and looked the car over. She'd had in mind a big black Mercedes like those she was used to seeing, but when her eyes lit on the little sports model, she squealed with delight. They went for a drive and that did it. When they got back, she threw her arms around her husband and thanked him for finding it. Then she finalized the deal with the owner. Mike watched as she wrote out a check for the entire purchase price.

She had her driver's license, she now had a car, and the next thing was to learn to drive it around the city. Newark was a zoo, so she was careful in the beginning, using maps and carefully reading street signs to reach her various destinations. In a short time, however, she was able to maneuver around quite confidently. She next began driving out to the lake by herself. Then she drove to the farm to see how things were going and to show off her car to her parents.

There everything was moving along nicely. The house construction was on schedule, the barns had been renovated, and the two horses were settling in comfortably. Often after parking the car and saying hello to her parents, Darlene would go jogging to keep herself trim. She worked her way up to doing five miles every day she was on the farm and wanted to maintain this routine when she was in the city. So she would get off work at one in the morning, hit the sack until about eight, and after a nice breakfast, she would run. She had worked out a suitable route that wound through the neighborhood. Part of the way was past bush land that had been set aside for a park.

One day when she was running by this area, she was startled to see Mike sitting in an old car by the side of the road reading the paper. She naturally stopped to see what was going on, but he was doing a stakeout of a nearby premises and didn't appreciate her drawing attention to the fact that he was there. So she got out of sight by getting into the car with him.

"Where did you get this rust bucket? It smells like your socks sometimes do."

"You aren't supposed to be in this car. What would happen if the man I'm waiting for showed up? You'd have to get out quick."

"I would, but in the meantime we can visit. I hardly ever see you since you started working days. Besides that you're always on a case someplace, and you're scarcely home. I miss you, darling, especially when I'm in bed trying to go to sleep."

"You can stay here," Mike relented, "but keep down. Pretend you are sleeping or something." So she huddled in the car, and they talked the morning away. All of a sudden Darlene, who had been feigning sleep, snapped awake. Walking on the road as far away from the car as possible was a man that she had seen the night before in the hospital. He had been lurking around outside of visiting hours and had eventually been chased out of the hospital by the security guards.

Darlene pointed him out to Mike, who had also spotted him. Mike said that the guy was one of the gang they were investigating but not the individual he was supposed to apprehend. He took note of what his wife said, asking her questions about her patients on the ward. The man clearly had been in the hospital for some reason, and tonight a police officer would go there to see what patient might be a person-of-interest to them.

Finally Darlene said good-bye and continued on with her run. She reflected that her husband seemed to have an easy job, sitting around reading the paper and jokingly told him so. However, she knew all too well that his job was, in reality, demanding and dangerous. She worried constantly about Mike when he was at work. Later when she was driving to the hospital, she drove past to check on him. The car was still there, and as she slowed he waved frantically for her to keep going, which she did.

She went on to work and waited for someone to come up and check on the patients on the ward. Two police officers came at what was supposed to be her mealtime, so she was almost half an hour late for that. She told them where the man had been lurking and they checked the patients in that area. To their delight and astonishment, a rough character on their list of wanted men was in one of the beds waiting for surgery. They called for backup and had him transferred immediately to the secured ward that was for convicts. He went with them, protesting all the way and yelling that the nurse who had turned him in was going to regret her actions.

When she got home after work, Mike was waiting up for her. They had a light snack, some wine, and then hit the sack, where he told her about his day's work. He informed her that when she had passed by in her car, he'd been almost ready to make an arrest. She hugged him and snuggled down beside him. As he continued to describe to her what he had been doing, she kissed his mouth closed so they could go to sleep.

It was mid-morning by the time Darlene pulled herself out of bed. Mike stayed behind, and she brought him coffee. It was so unusual to have her husband home when she was home that she got back into bed, and they drank their coffees while they talked about their jobs. Mike loved his little Muscovite dearly and couldn't get enough of her ever. However, he was involved in an ongoing drug investigation that consumed most of his time and had for several months. He would be up for promotion to detective in the near future and desperately wanted to prove himself.

She didn't do her regular run. Instead, they hung around the apartment enjoying each other until they both had to go to work. That was Mike: sometimes he'd work days and then a string of nights with no regular schedule. She could never tell when she would get a chance to be with him, so when the opportunity came, everything else went on the back burner. When she got to work, there was a message for her in her box at the nursing station. She thought nothing of it until she opened the single sheet of paper. Then she went white as a ghost. The message said, "PREPARE TO DIE LITTLE RUSKIE NURSE. YOU DID SOMETHING WHEN YOU SHOULD HAVE MINDED YOUR OWN BUSINESS & YOU'LL GET WHAT'S COMING TO YOU REAL SOON!"

Darlene grabbed the counter to hold herself up and showed the letter to Irene, the head nurse. Irene read it and immediately dialed the police station. Darlene was asked if she wanted to do her shift and she replied, "I'll stay of course." She began her work, but her hands were shaking so much that she had to get another nurse to help her administer medications — needles were out of the question. But she managed until the police came to talk to her. After that she felt better but intended to follow every bit of advice they gave her. She left work only when Mike dropped by to escort her to her vehicle. He watched her drive home, and his heart went out to her. If he lost her, he didn't know what he'd do. Those kinds of thoughts went through his mind while he went back to work, but he could hardly keep his mind on what he was doing. He began to think that work was taking up too much of their lives. They needed to spend more time together.

Back at the station, he too received a hand-scrawled message sent by fax to the police department and addressed to him. It said, "YOU CAN'T WALK HER TO HER CAR EVERY TIME. KISS YOUR WIFE GOOD-BYE. IF NOT TONIGHT THEN SOME OTHER TIME."

It was unsigned and deeply disturbing. Mike knew that somebody had been waiting for Darlene when she got off work, and that they were serious about their intentions. He had a long discussion with his superiors about the situation and they wrung their hands over the matter, but nobody thought about the fact that Darlene carried a gun.

When Darlene got home, she carefully parked the car and then scurried up to the apartment. After a hot cuppa, she got out her little gun and cleaned it thoroughly, taking her time about it, to make sure that every piece was absolutely clean. Then she oiled it and tested the action several times to make sure that it worked smoothly. Satisfied, she returned it to the holster, which she'd also oiled, and practiced getting at it quickly. She could do no more for the moment. Unless they just shot her from a concealed position, she would put up one hell of a fight.

The following night when she got off work at one in the morning, she walked to her car in the midst of a group of other people who watched her until she was actually in her car. That was one night. Mike had told her about the message he had received, and they were taking each night as it came. There was no problem getting one of the security team to walk her to her car, which she did on other nights. Her gun was in a holster under her jacket. She always wore a jacket of some kind, even on the warmest of evenings. Hardly anyone knew that she carried a gun, and she took extreme caution all the time.

While she enjoyed working the evening shift, she knew that she could use her seniority to switch to days. The afternoon shift was the busiest and the hardest on staff and nurses, and because she was always on the go, the time just flew by. She decided against working the day shift.

One night about three weeks after she received the warning letter, she stepped out of the hospital door with two other nurses. She felt quite safe but had barely started down the concrete steps after them when she was grabbed from behind. Her arms were held in a vice grip and she could do nothing. She could have screamed, which would have alerted the other two nurses, but instead she dropped to her knees, which caused the attacker to loosen his grip on her arms. She then rolled down the stairs and on to her back. She had her gun now, and the attacker, who was rushing towards, her received a shot in the stomach. A second man was coming down the stairs and pointing a gun at her. She fired, but missed and hit a porch light. She fired again just as the man squeezed off a shot. He missed but landed on top of her with half his face missing.

She lay still for a few moments, and then took huge gasps of air as she began struggling to get up. There was blood all over her jacket from the second man. Someone told her that the police were on their way and helped her get out from under the body. She got on her knees; then she forced herself up. A black woman's voice said,

"Darling, where'd you get that thing?" Darlene realized that she was still holding the gun in her shaking hand. She immediately slipped it back into the holster and only then noticed the dark stains on her jacket. She'd have to buy a new one, and for some reason, this seemed terribly important. Darlene realized she was going into shock. Someone helped her up the stairs and into the hospital. They guided her to a chair and she realized that she was in the hands of the police. She couldn't help herself and began to cry. One of the officers handed her some tissues and asked her for her gun. She took a good look at the speaker to make sure he was a cop, then she handed over her piece and requested that he call Mike Strong to the hospital.

"Is Mike a friend of yours?"

"He's my husband. I think that he should be here if he can make it."

"So do I ma'am. We'll put out a call for him now." Darlene collected herself and began answering questions. She had two good witnesses, the two nurses who had been just a few feet ahead of her when she came out the door. She was describing the written threats just as Mike showed up. He stood looking at her in shock and relief.

He'd only gotten a report on the way to the ER, and all the way to the hospital, he had feared the worst. He grabbed her, gave her a bear hug, and told her everything was going to be all right. Then he knelt by her chair while the questioning continued.

Mike kept butting in to provide answers to questions that she was asked. The other cop politely but firmly told Mike to find a chair a convenient distance away, and Mike reluctantly retreated.

When the questioning was finished, Mike drove her home. He said that they'd pick up her car the next day. She was only allowed to go because she was Mike's wife, and because they knew that she'd be available when required. She wasn't off the hook, but it was fairly clear that she had been acting in self-defense.

When Mike got her home, they went up and she had a good shot of straight whiskey. Mike was watching her. Finally, he said to her, "The officer said that you seemed to be pretty cool in the situation, and that you knew how to defend yourself. How do you feel about it now?"

"I'm fine. I just want to go to bed and get some rest." She looked at him steadily.

"You can sleep after that? After what you've just been through?"

"Sure, Dear. You can go finish your shift. I'll be just fine."

Mike couldn't help himself. He stared at her in horror. Some police officers had to take time off after killing somebody, and it was a risk of their job. His wife was going to just go to bed and sleep after killing two people. He was incredulous and asked her again if she was sure that she wasn't still in shock, but Darlene again told him to go back to work and then shooed him out the door. When he was gone, she reflexively reached for her gun to clean it when she remembered that the police had it. Well, she'd just get a back-up gun in the morning. She went to bed and to sleep.

Mike went straight to the police station. The officer that was handling the case was there making out a report when Mike walked in.

"Hi Mike. I thought you'd stay with your wife for tonight; she must be pretty upset."

"She said she was going to get some sleep. She doesn't seem to be bothered at all by what went down. Have you ever seen anybody like that before?"

"You mean cool? Sure. She was pretty cool when I questioned her. She's a good kid. If you're back on duty, Barney wants to see you." Mike went back to work, but his mind was on Darlene. Cool!

She was the Ice Lady to beat them all. He couldn't help but start thinking about the other two men that she was suspected of killing. The case had never been closed, and while she had never been questioned about it, Mike figured she was a prime suspect. Naturally he didn't share his thought with anyone in the department. But now, he was even surer that she had killed before. Otherwise why had her first gun ended up in the lake? She was too smart and too careful to lose it there accidentally. He hadn't pressed her about it then or later, but it had never been laid to rest in his mind. Now, black thoughts rose to haunt him.

Darlene turned up for work as scheduled the next day. The head nurse did a double take and then stared.

"I didn't think you'd make it in today, not after last night!"

Darlene just smiled. "You can't keep a good nurse down I guess…." She smiled again. Irene simply looked at her like she had two heads.

"You can go back home if you want to. You don't have to work after what happened. I was told by Personnel that you wouldn't be in today. If you're going to work I'll have to send Betty back downstairs."

"I'm here to work. There's nothing wrong with me. I couldn't just sit at home doing nothing. Send her back downstairs." She started her duties while Irene the head nurse went to find Betty. All shift, Darlene kept being interrupted while trying to work. The chief administrator of the hospital dropped by to ask how she was doing. Then several other hospital officials came by, and she could hardly get anything done. Nobody could understand how she could blow two people away and just keep right on going. For herself, Darlene found their reactions puzzling but tried to say as little as possible.

When she got off work that night, Mike was there to escort her home. He gave her an update on what the department was doing about her case. She was considered to have acted solely in self-defense, and there was little likelihood that any police officers would bother her anymore about it. However, as a formality, she was required to come to the station in the morning and complete an affidavit concerning the entire episode.

"You know, honey, I've never killed anybody in the line of duty, and I've been on the force eight years. How does it feel to do something like that?"

"It doesn't bother me." She shrugged. "I was just protecting myself. It was me or them." Mike didn't say anything. There was nothing he could say that wouldn't antagonize or irritate her. He wanted to ask her about the two men that had been killed near her place a couple of years ago, but he knew that to do it would invite her anger, and he couldn't bring himself to do that.

In no time life was back to normal. She went out every morning on her way home from work expecting to be attacked, but nothing more ever happened. There were no more messages left for her or Mike. He now knew that he could count on her to be careful, and if that didn't work, he could count on her to be a survivalist.

A few months later, while Darlene was doing her shift, Mike took a bullet to the shoulder. It happened at about five in the morning, and she was called at the hospital to be told that her husband had been admitted to the ER with a gunshot wound. The head nurse told her to go check on her husband and to take her time. The doctor recognized her and briefly filled her in. He said that it was a very small wound that had torn some muscle but went right on through. He said that her husband would probably be off work for about three months while it healed. She couldn't see him right away because he was sedated, but she went back at the end of her shift and talked with him for a bit. He was to be in the hospital overnight.

When he came home from the hospital, she took a couple of days off to take care of him. This proved to be needless because aside from a weak shoulder he was fine. They discussed the dangers of his line of work, but he said that he was a police officer and would remain one as long as he could.

He said that it was just the luck of the draw and others had suffered more than he had while working. That didn't make her feel any better. She was worried about him all the time, and now she'd worry even more.

When he began to feel better, he started spending time out at the farm fixing things. His shoulder needed exercise, and he did that regularly, but the rest of the time he was building fences and coming up with other DIY projects. Darlene saw less of him than when he was working. She practically had to go out to the farm if she wanted to see him at all. He, on the other hand, was having tea every morning with Dolly, Darlene's mother. She and her husband Fred took full advantage of Mike's being there to get to know him better. As he sat sipping tea one day, Dolly began reminiscing about Darlene's childhood, and it wasn't too long before Mike was asking why she was under investigation for murder in Russia.

Dolly joked about him all of a sudden becoming a policeman with her but explained that Darlene was simply wanted for questioning about the murder of a man that she had nursed.

"The man was a diamond merchant." he added innocently, "so plenty of people might have wanted to rob him."

"A diamond merchant?" Mike asked in a barely audible whisper. "Yes. He bought and sold diamonds. He was supposed to have had quite a few in his safe but when they opened it the safe was empty." She looked at Mike quietly wondering why he wanted to know about such things.

"Do you have any idea how much money Darlene has?"

"No. You should know, you're her husband."

"She has never told me just how much money she has, but she seems to have plenty. Did she leave Russia with lots of money?"

His mother-in-law's face closed up and she said, "Maybe we shouldn't talk about these things. I think I'll talk to Darlene about it first." The conversation ended on that note. Mike decided that he could easily enough find out if Darlene had brought a bunch of diamonds into the country. The problem was, did he really want to know?

The next time he and Darlene were having a meal, he looked at her, wondering as he had so many times before, just who she was. He'd reached the point where he couldn't let the matter rest although the answer might break up their marriage. He told her that he had been talking to her mother about her childhood and teen years. She smiled, relaxed and happy to be with him, and Mike lost his nerve. He didn't tell her the direction that the conversation had gone and wondered why he couldn't just accept her as she was even if that included a few mysteries.

Mike could easily have scoured the pawnshops for diamonds during his working hours. Doing so would be quite legitimate because the diamonds would have been smuggled into the country, which was a serious offense on it's own. He passed pawnshops every day when at work and thought of his little Muscovite every time. However, he didn't go on a concentrated search for information about a large quantity of diamonds being pawned. He couldn't bring himself to do it. What would he do if he found out that the light of his world was a murderer and thief? Where would his marriage be? Mike believed in being married for life. He also believed in trust and honesty. Torn about what to do, he just could not bring himself to play cop with his wife's past.

Their marriage didn't suffer from his doubts; he hid his thoughts and theories well. He loved his wife and demonstrated that love every chance he got. When they spent time at the lake together, he never mentioned the loss of her gun. At the farm they enjoyed riding and gardening or just lazing around.

He never said anything about the fact that her mother didn't think she had any money, while she owned such expensive pieces of property. He avoided anything that might jeopardize the tight bond that held them together. Darlene had not the slightest clue that Mike knew or thought such things about her.

Darlene's birthday was in May, and one year, to her utter amazement, Mike bought her a lighter model Harley Davidson motorcycle. She looked at it sitting there in the farm driveway, all black and chrome and giggled. What, she wondered, was she supposed to do with that? The answer quickly became clear, as Mike announced he would be teaching her how to ride. He had purchased a leather outfit, a helmet, and gloves for her, so she knew he was serious. Mike was an experienced rider because of his work, loved riding, and wanted her to learn so that they could also do this together. At first, Darlene could barely handle even this smaller model because she was so petite, but she obediently followed his instructions, and within a week she had enough confidence to try for her road license.

When she was classified as roadworthy, Mike got one of the bikes from the station and they went out to the farm. When Darlene sailed into the yard on her motorcycle, her mother nearly fainted. She came running out screaming at her daughter and wondering what "the youngsters" would be up to next.

She still hadn't talked to her daughter about money and asked Mike to wait until she did. She didn't intend to start something and hoped that her son-in-law would let matters rest. For the time being, Mike was willing to do that even though he knew that the longer he put it off the colder the trail became. In his heart he hoped that he would never uncover that part of his wife's past, and that the trail would vanish forever. He practically vowed to himself that he'd never set foot in a pawnshop again if it meant finding out that Darlene had unloaded a bunch of diamonds.

10

It had been bothering Darlene for a while that they were paying rent on an apartment when they could instead be paying a mortgage on their own house. She finally had the opportunity tospeak with Mike about it, but he was lukewarm to the idea of moving. The apartment was well-appointed and comfortable. It was reasonably well located so that both could get to work without major discomfort. If they bought a house, it would have to be both farther from the hospital and the police station. Since Mike was back to working odd, usually long, hours, and was always on call, it seemed reasonable to remain nearby instead of out in the suburbs. However he said he'd think about it.

Now that she had brought it up, she wondered if Mike would look around for a house that would suit them. She spoke about how they would have more room for the bikes, perhaps a basement, and a yard rather than a simple balcony.

Suggesting they move into a house was in fact the first spoke in the wheel she was building: she wanted to have children. Darlene was a good nurse but didn't envision spending her entire life in that career. She wanted to be a homemaker, a housewife, and a mother. Although she wasn't as yet in a hurry to accomplish these things, she was planting seeds for the future.

11

One night, Mike was holding Darlene's hand and admiring the distinctive shape of her slender fingers. An urge suddenly overcame him, and he asked impulsively, "Do you think thisis a small diamond?" He was referring to the diamond in her engagement ring.

She took her time before answering, knowing what disaster might develop if she simply blurted out something without careful consideration.

"It is a nice-sized diamond, Mike darling. It's just what I wanted. And besides, a ring is just a ring, but I have you as well — better than any diamond. Mike accepted her response with a squeeze around the shoulders. Why pursue the subject? Her body felt warm against his, and he wanted it to remain that way. She giggled and turned her face to his.

Darlene had a real estate agent, a woman who understood her, and was always ready to help. With Wendy's assistance, Darlene had been able to find their apartment, the house she rented to May, and the farm. Now she went to Wendy again and talked about a house in the suburbs, something with two or three bedrooms, a large yard, and either a work area, or a basement that could be made into a work area. It could be a fixer-upper because both Darlene and Mike liked to putter around, fixing things. Once she had Wendy on the job, Darlene spent her free time cruising around looking at the houses that Wendy suggested. Success was not immediate. She couldn't say exactly what was missing until one day she sat on her bike, eyeing yet another forlorn-looking piece of property. The yard was large but bare of grass or trees or anything. TREES! That's what she wanted. She motored back to the real estate office and left a message for Wendy that she wanted a house with trees in the yard. Preferably lots of trees.

She didn't tell Mike that she was looking at houses. It wasn't yet time. For his part, he hadn't brought the subject up since she had mentioned it, which meant that he wasn't keen on moving out of the apartment. But, Darlene would start working on him once she had found a suitable property. Then she would have something to show him and could broach the subject of her long-range plans. Not all of them at once, but at least some of them for now. She didn't want to frighten him, just give him a little nudge forwards.

She had no difficulty seeing herself playing with a little daughter on a nice lawn. But she wondered how Mike would view that picture. She had no plans just yet to tell him that she wanted to get pregnant. However, it was a wonder that he didn't figure it out for himself. Why else would she want a house with a yard?

When Mike went back to work after the shooting, he was on desk duty for six months. During that whole time, Darlene felt wonderful. She didn't have to worry that he wouldn't come home at night, and she relaxed. She even began to gain some of her weight back; after their near arrest in Russia, she had lost several pounds from stress and anxiety.

When he went back on the road, he left for work at eight in the morning and got home at two a.m. Darlene beat him home by half an hour. One evening he looked absolutely beat. He had been on a stake-out during the early part of the night and then had participated in a police raid of a rooming house where some drug dealers were operating. It had been a long shift, but mostly it had been dangerous. The dealers had better weapons than the cops, as usual, but fortunately this time they didn't get a chance to use them.

Darlene adored Mike. She knew that he loved his work, and she couldn't imagine what kind of work he'd do instead. When they'd first been married, she had loved his work too but had grown to hate it. During the time that Mike was off the streets, one of his colleagues had lost her leg because someone put a bullet in it. Another cop was killed, and one was in hospital recovering from gunshot wounds. Darlene hated it every time Mike walked out the door because she didn't know if she'd ever see him again. She wanted Mike's baby so that if he did get killed, she'd at least have someone to remember him by.

Wendy had some difficulty finding a house that excited Darlene. She had put the real estate woman on it in the early spring. Darlene had looked at house after house, and it was now almost autumn. At last Wendy phoned with good news.

Wendy gave her the address of a house on a corner lot and suggested she have a ride by. She cruised past the house on her bike, then parked to take a better look. It was big, set back from the road and partially hidden by trees. A lane led up to the house and altogether it looked like a little bit of country in the middle of the city. Darlene rode by it a couple more times and then went down the lane behind it. There were trees in the back, too. Tall deciduous trees, leafy in the summer, and making a multi-colored carpet to rake in the fall. Trees that she could put a swing on for her little Mikey. She finally rode home and told Wendy that she'd like to see the inside of the house.

When Darlene next saw Mike, she enthusiastically told him about the house she had looked at in the suburbs. Mike listened patiently as she told him of the condition of the house, the beauty of the lot, and whatever else she could think of. He agreed to go with her to have a look at it, and they set a time. Darlene communicated the time to Wendy, who made arrangements with the occupants to show the house.

Mike was anything but enthusiastic about moving. He thought that he had made himself clear on the subject, but he hadn't counted on his wife's persistence. But after he saw the property, had a look at the inside of the house, and listened as she painted a picture of domestic bliss, his heart softened. She finally told him that she wanted to become a housewife with a bunch of children to take care of. His reaction amazed even him. He found that he too would like to have some youngsters that he could help raise.

After they toured the property, and he had seen all there was to see, they retreated to their apartment to discuss the venture.

"I don't suppose that money is any problem." Mike said in a sarcastic but humorous voice. Darlene just looked at him. She knew the bait he was dangling, and she wasn't going to bite.

"We could handle it with a good down payment and a mortgage payment equal to our rent. I guess that I could put up the down payment if I had to."

"Yes, I suppose our finances might get confusing if we both contribute to purchasing the place instead of just one of us?" He was sarcastic again, only this time there was an edge to his remark.

"Mike, darling...." She put her arms around him giving him a big hug. He knew that if they were indeed arguing, he had just lost. They sat down at the kitchen table and began working out an offer on the house.

If the offer was accepted, they would have to wait three months before they could take possession of the property. That would make moving in sort of like a Christmas present for them. Mike thought about having to drive or ride in from the suburbs every day, and it didn't sit well, but he knew that they had definitely outgrown the apartment. He was glad that he had bought himself a Harley- Davidson. He could use that to go to work and save money. Mike believed in being frugal, as did Darlene. She was in fact a penny pincher extraordinaire about most purchases. But when it came to making good solid investments, she let the money flow. The farm was paid for, her house was paid for, and now they would be putting their rent payment into their own house instead. The only property that wasn't solely in her name was the house where she intended to be a housewife. That was in both their names because his paycheck was going to be the source of each month's payment. Darlene had made a very substantial down payment

"Some time," Mike said to himself, "I'm going to find out just how much money she has even if I don't ever find out where she got it from."

They moved in on December tenth. Darlene supervised the move by being at the apartment while the movers loaded up. Her mother was at the house to receive everything. After that it would be up to Mike and Darlene to unpack and make the place livable. They did that slowly over the next couple of weeks. Both of them were computer literate, so they began by using the extra bedroom as the computer room. It was a tremendous relief to get all that stuff out of the living room, which was where it had been in the apartment.

The ground was frozen, snow was piled high all over the yard, and the trees were bare of leaves. Darlene drove in driving her Mercedes, and Mike used his car to go to work. They saw even less of each other than when they were in the apartment, but now Darlene was off the pill.

She hoped that it wouldn't be long before she became a stay-at-home mom. In the meantime both of them put money away against the mortgage and paved the way for a successful future. Mike really didn't want to pry into his wife's affairs when it came to money. She gladly shared the financial burdens that they had and paid her way many times over. What more could he ask? It didn't really matter where the money was coming from, as long as they didn't go overboard. It was quite obvious to her husband that she knew how to handle money and get the most for every dollar. When she needed advice she readily came to Mike for his opinion.

When the leaves started to come out on the tall shade trees in the yard, the doctor told Darlene that she was indeed in the family way. Darlene intended to work three-quarter time until just before she was due. Then she was going to take on motherhood. Dolly could hardly keep up with what her daughter was doing at the best of times, but now she couldn't believe that her little girl was a real estate tycoon of sorts. Dolly Milanovich had lived her whole life in a rented shack. Her daughter owned a house and a farm plus had half ownership in another house. Truly, America was a land of opportunity.

12

While Frank and Wanda were their closest friends, Frank wasn't the only cop that called the Strong's place a second home; there were cops around often sitting arounddrinking beer or coffee and talking shop. Darlene was used to Mike having three other guys in the living room for half the day while she found an excuse to be elsewhere. They all knew her and accepted her, but they came to talk with Mike. The only difference in Wanda's case was that her and Frank came out to the farm to run, ski or enjoy the solitude. The four of them went camping together, on picnics, and often they would all sleep at the same residence, sometimes for days on end.

Mike enjoyed the company of his pals and needed that outlet. Having the house meant that there was the garage where they could hang out if Darlene was using the house. Or they could sit in the back yard in the summer time and almost pretend they were in the country. Sometimes the cops would come on their bikes, and then Darlene knew that they'd all head out for a run to someplace that she didn't know about and be gone all day. Life wasn't all work either for Mike or for Darlene, and they began to enjoy this new pace.

Darlene began getting bigger. Her workload was lightened, and she began talking about when she wouldn't be working at the hospital anymore. Her workmates envied her up to a point. Many of them had already been through it all and could only wish her luck. The ones who knew of her house that was rented out to nurses were envious but only of her wealth. They would not have been so jealous had they known its source.

It was late fall when the hospital informed Darlene that she was being laid off. She was simply too close to her time for any risks to be taken with her condition and the hospital had to think of its liability. She had a going-away party one afternoon, said her good-bye's, and left the hospital vowing never to return except as a patient. Awkwardly maneuvering herself into her car, she drove home reflecting happily on the opening of a new phase of her life. She was looking forward to it even more than she had originally thought.

She knew that it would be a miracle if Mike was anywhere nearby when she had to go to the hospital. They discussed the matter thoroughly and decided that she would use a taxi service to get to the hospital and then try to contact Mike.

Within a week Darlene went into labor. All went like clockwork except for contacting Mike. He was out on the road involved in a delicate situation and couldn't be interrupted. When he finally was reached, he was the proud father of a tiny baby girl. Darlene remained in the hospital for just one further day to make sure everything was working properly, then was discharged. She went home with the assurance that a care worker would call within two days to check up on her. Darlene's mother, Dolly, came to stay with her for a week while she got back on her feet and the baby settled in.

The baby was born during that part of Mike's career when he was often involved in "sensitive" operations. He would be gone for long periods of time while he worked undercover or on almost "secret" missions. Hardly anyone in the department seemed to know anything about what exactly he and his team were doing. At least they wouldn't discuss it with Darlene, no matter how well they knew her and liked her.

She tried to find out how dangerous his work was, but he wouldn't discuss that with her either. He would only say that it was very unlikely that anything disastrous could happen to him during the course of his duties. He was non-committal but tried to make up for it by being attentive and as much help as possible when he was at home. He learned how to change diapers, how to prepare a formula, and what to do when little Victoria cried. It was a joint decision to call the little girl Victoria. There was no particular attachment to the name, it was simply that they both liked it.

Dianne Foster came to visit Darlene. She was the wife of Nick Foster, who was a good friend of Mike's and a friend of Darlene's also. Dianne had come to spend the day helping Darlene cope with taking care of the new baby. She had three children and had lots of good tips to pass on. That was the beginning of an almost endless stream of police officers' wives who dropped by to help Darlene out. When they'd had an open house party to celebrate moving to the suburbs, the house was full of cops and nurses who spent the evening enjoying each others' company thoroughly. Darlene was also called upon by a number of her friends from the hospital. Once in a while one of her visitors would end up spending the night, especially if both their husbands were working. There was a general sense of camaraderie between the nurses and police officers because occasionally they ended up working together.

One morning Mike got home somewhere between two and three a.m. He had left for work at seven the previous morning and felt tired, cranky, and tense. Parking his car in the driveway, he began to get out. As the car door opened, a volley of shots rang out splattering the door with bullets. Mike hit the floor of the car digging frantically for his gun. More shots came at him and he rapidly returned fire.

Darlene was at home with the baby, both asleep and a woman named Primrose was sleeping in the guest room. A friend of Darlene's through Mike, she was staying over while her own husband was at work chasing down criminals. They both awoke with a start and the house was soon flooded with lights.

Outside, the firing stopped and a car peeled away. Mike pulled himself together, and after some hesitation started across the dark yard. Halfway across he stumbled over something and landed on his face. Cursing he got up and was startled to see it was a body. He had shot and killed one of the attackers. Mike kneeled down and checked for a pulse. Definitely dead. From his car he radioed headquarters to initiate the cleanup; then he went into the house.

Darlene was standing by the kitchen stove away from all the windows in her gown. Primrose was sitting by the table wearing one of Mike's bathrobes. Both looked scared. Darlene ran to Mike and nearly tackled him with one of her bear hugs. He returned the gesture and said, "The police will be here shortly, dear. There's a body on our front lawn. I guess I've killed someone." Darlene knew that the house would probably be full of cops before they were through so she put on a pot of coffee.

"You shot him?"

"I think so. We'll have to wait until the coroner and the others arrive and we can have ballistics check the bullets before I know for sure." Red lights flashed from the driveway and he went back outside.

Soon the yard was bright as day while the officers went about their work. It turned out that Mike hadn't shot the man; he had been dumped there by the attackers. The man was a stool pigeon who had been co-operating with the police. He had apparently been found out and killed.

The attackers had dumped him on the lawn of Mike Strong's house as a defiant gesture or possibly a warning.

A couple of officers told Mike that there were four bullet holes in his car door and that it was a miracle that he hadn't been hit during the skirmish. They sat sipping hot black coffee while they took down Mike's statement. One of them told Mike that he should take a few extra hours off seeing as he was still up at such a late hour. It was decided that Mike wouldn't appear for work until the next afternoon. Eventually everybody was gone. The coroner had removed the body and the cops had left. In the house everybody went to bed but Mike couldn't sleep. There were a few things he hadn't told anyone about the victim. One was that the man had been under deep cover in the police department and wasn't a stool but rather, an undercover police officer who was so well concealed that nobody should ever have been able to ferret him out. The fact that somebody had found him out meant that Mike's whole investigation was in jeopardy. Dumping the body at Mike's home was an explicit warning to him, and he knew that, but nobody else did. Whether or not he would reveal this to his partners was a question he had to deal with. He could never tell Darlene the whole truth about the night's catastrophe. He had to tell her that not only he, but she and the baby could possibly be in serious danger.

When he finally did get to sleep, Mike slept almost the clock around. Darlene hovered over him like a mother hen. She was a tiny little mite, but she had strength and a sense of protection which she directed towards the safety of her family. She would not stand by and let harm come to Mike if she could in any way help it. When he got up, Mike tried to pretend that every thing was fine and nobody had to worry, but Darlene knew better. Somebody didn't dump a body on their lawn just for the fun of it. She told Mike that she knew the whole family was now in danger and that they should, as a family, act as if they knew that. Mike could only agree.

They decided that for a while it might be better if Darlene and Victoria went to the farm and stayed with her mother. There was plenty of room, the criminals might not know about the farm and Mike could worry less about his wife when he was at work. They spent as much time as they could together that day but when Mike returned to work, Darlene left for the farm. Primrose had already left that morning.

Further investigation concluded that Mike had probably interrupted the criminals while they were dumping the body. It was thought that they hadn't exactly been there to take shots at Mike, but since he showed up they decided to get in a few licks. This fit in with how Mike saw the picture also. He had just been unlucky. On the other hand, they may have tried to do something to Darlene and the baby, so perhaps his arrival had been fortunate after all.

13

There were now nine horses on the twenty acres that Darlene owned. Two of the horses belonged to Mike and Darlene. The other ones belonged to neighbors and city folk who paidto have them pastured and stabled. There was a large barn full of hay for the horses in the wintertime. Fred was capable of shoeing horses and did any of that work as required. He was also responsible for seeing that the horses were well-fed and healthy. On one of the two acreages, there was a paddock for the horses where people could ride. The fencing was white plank, which made the operation look very elegant and upscale. Mike and Darlene had done much of the work on the farm themselves and hired people to do the rest.

They were also building a new house on the ten-acre lot where Darlene intended to rent it to people who had horses they wanted to train. Darlene now had friends that owned, showed and raced horses so she had people who were interested even before the house was completed. Although normally confident, she felt somewhat intimidated at times by the horse people that she dealt with. There was no doubt in her mind that little Victoria would grow up familiar with horses in every way. She would have her own horse as soon as she was old enough to care for it. Darlene had no idea how to care for a horse, but Fred did, and he could impart his knowledge to his granddaughter.

Mike got out to the farm as often as possible to spend time with his wife and daughter. He was, however, obviously under a great deal of stress, but couldn't talk about what was bothering him because it was work related. He did say that Darlene should stay at the farm for a while and even there, try not to stand out She was worried about Mike. Worried that he was putting himself in danger, that he was working too hard and too many long hours on the job. He was way overdue for a vacation, but there wasn't even one on the horizon. All Darlene could do was teach her mother how to play cards, and wait.

14

It was late spring. Darlene and Victoria were out watching ducks floating around on a large pond that had gathered on the grounds from the melting snow. Darlene made up her mind that comesummer, there would be a man-made pond with domesticated ducks. She was sitting on a rock, and Victoria was standing nearby when Dolly called from the house that there was a phone call. The tone of Dolly's voice hinted that it wasn't an ordinary call. Darlene gathered her child and headed for the house.

Darlene hadn't heard from Mike for three days. She knew that he was heavily involved, but it was seldom that they didn't see each other or at least talk each day. She took the phone from Dolly.

"Hello?"

"Hello. Is this Darlene?"

"Yes. Who is calling?"

"I'm Captain James Crook, one of Mike's superior officers. Mike has had a slight accident, an automobile accident. He's in the hospital and will be there for about a week."

"Can I go to see him?"

"I'm afraid not. It is a delicate situation and you are to remain where you are, keeping a low profile. You are not to leave the farm for any reason. It is for your safety that I say this."

"What happened to Mike? Am I in danger out here?"

"You aren't in any danger that we know of so far. Mike was run off the road by people who tried to kill him. I wouldn't tell *anyone* that if I were you. I shouldn't be telling you, but we know you have good sense. He has no broken bones but maybe a slight concussion. His car is a write-off."

"Can I phone him?"

"No. For security reasons, we'll phone you at an agreed upon time each day with an update. When would be a good time for you?"

"How about ten o'clock every morning?"

"Fine. Mrs. Strong, we'll call you each day at ten in the morning until further notice. Once he's discharged, Mike will be off work for a while and out there with you. Then we're going to relieve him of his present duties because these people are serious about trying to kill him, and if they knew where you were, they'd probably try for you too. I understand you are familiar with weapons. You should try to keep one handy and if you can, get some practice in."

"Thank you for calling. I don't know what to say. Tell Mike I love him."

"Will do. We'll call you tomorrow. 'Bye for now."

When Darlene hung up the phone her senses were piqued. She went to her bedroom and got her gun. Right in front of Dolly, she checked the loads and then slipped the holster on. Dolly watched her questioningly. Darlene gave a brief version of what the phone call had been about. She said very little, just that Mike was in the hospital, and that everyone on the farm should be particularly careful because some people might try to bother them. She didn't elaborate.

Every day someone called Darlene from the station, a different man each time. Once Frank called, but he was as guarded as anyone and wouldn't tell her more than she already knew. At the end of a week, a black limo pulled into the farmyard and Mike got out. He stood on shaky legs and looked around. Someone got a large suitcase out of the car and walked toward the house. Darlene saw them coming and ran out into Mike's arms.

She could tell that he was weak and offered her shoulder to help him into the house. The driver set the suitcase down and waited. Mike thanked him, they exchanged a few words, and the man left.

Darlene had the coffee pot on and offered Mike a cup. While he sipped his coffee she surveyed him anxiously. He looked pale and thin and utterly exhausted despite his stay in the hospital. When he had finished the coffee, she helped him into the bedroom and onto the bed. He complained that he'd been lying around for the past week but then sank back on the pillows like he nonetheless needed the rest. She got on the bed beside him, and while they hugged each other, he told her what happened.

He had been driving his Volvo in the suburb of Ashfield and happened to go past a bush area where there was a steep bank. Suddenly there was a car behind him almost pushing him along, and then a station wagon came alongside him and ran him off the road. He went over the edge but his car slid down the hill in the mud instead of rolling as they had expected it to. Had it rolled, he wouldn't be alive, but as it was, his car smashed headlong into a large tree that destroyed the car. The windshield was smashed, and Mike had sustained a severe blow to the head. The doctors had found a concussion, in fact. Mike had had his cellular along and had called 911 before passing out.

The emergency crew was there in less than five minutes, but his car had gone down about a hundred feet, and it was difficult to get him back up on the roadway. When they discovered who they had on the stretcher, one of the nurses suggested that Darlene be notified right away, but the police took charge and in the end this wasn't done until morning. The attack on him happened at about 3 a.m. He'd been out in his own vehicle at that time of morning because he had gotten off work an hour earlier and had invited one of his buddies to come to his place. The officer came and they'd had a few drinks. Then Mike offered to drive him home because he didn't have his own car with him. He had been returning from the other officer's home when he was attacked. It was assumed that the attackers had followed him, waiting for a good opportunity to kill him and had nearly succeeded.

"What's going to happen to our house seeing as we're both out here?" asked Darlene.

"Oh, I have let it to four guys from an army base who want to live off-base. They're commandos and carry machine guns. They are renting it cheap in return for protecting the property from any vandals or saboteurs. We'll remain out here until I am able to go back to work, and then I believe that they are going to give me my vacation time. I think that I'll get two months vacation since I haven't had one for so long."

"Then what?"

"I was thinking that we'd all go back to the Bahamas and stay at the place we stayed in for our honeymoon. I'd like to take Victoria with us. I think it's something that's overdue." He put his arm tighter around Darlene and began to nod off. When he was completely asleep, she untangled herself and crept out of the bedroom, returning to the kitchen, where she picked up her two-year-old daughter and hugged the child to her breast.

The days passed slowly. It was a time of recuperation for Mike and with the help of Dolly's large healthy meals, Mike gained weight and got his color back.

He took Darlene out to the pasture where they both shot at tin cans for practice. Darlene hadn't paid much attention to her gun use since she'd left work, and she was rusty. Mike guided her through a refresher course to the point where she was once more capable of defending herself under any circumstances.

After that, Mike dug out the rifles and got Darlene started on learning to shoot them properly. He had three different hunting rifles but never intended to use them for hunting anything but people. One was a .22, one was a .30-30 and the other was an M-16. He put up a proper target at a distance of 300 yards and showed her how to zero in on the bull's eye at that distance. They spent several afternoons on this before she began to feel that she could put up a good fight with these weapons.

For three months there was virtually no contact with the department aside from an occasional visit by one of the brass. Mike's paycheck kept on coming regularly, and his condition was monitored by a medical examiner. He had to undergo physiotherapy for a while and then submit to several types of examinations before he was finally classified ready to return to work. They were in no hurry to put him back in the harness and just as he had predicted, they gave him six weeks of vacation with pay. He immediately booked seats with a travel agent, and in a few days the three of them were on their way to the tropics.

True to plan, they got rooms in the same villa where they had spent their honeymoon. It was a waterfront location and the first thing that Mike wanted to do was go to the beach with Victoria and let her become acquainted with the warm water lapping her feet. She squealed with delight and they spent quality time in the sun. When it had cooled a little in the evening, they sipped beer and dined on local shrimp and fruits. Later, they went for a walk and gazed at the huge silver moon that flooded the sky. Darlene was happier than she had been in a very long time.

They stayed for a month before returning to the cooler temperatures of Newark. As soon as she could slip away, Darlene went to see her doctor, who confirmed that yes indeed she was once again pregnant. She swelled with pure joy and could hardly wait to get home to tell Mike, where he was engaged in an intense game of cards with Dolly. Darlene had to wait until she could get him alone before she imparted the news.

When she told him, he too was thrilled for her and them.

"I hope it's a boy this time." he gushed. She just giggled and hugged him tenderly.

15

While they'd been away, the insurance money for his car arrived and they went shopping for a new one. They were under strict orders not to show their faces around the inner city, which limited them to using dealerships in the valley. They checked out several different kinds of vehicles before their attention was turned to a wagon type that they could use to haul the kids around. They agreed that it was time to get a family vehicle that they could use to go on trips.

After they purchased the van, they immediately took off across the Midwestern states on a trial run in their new vehicle. They packed it with everything that they could think of and went from one motel to another, sight-seeing and enjoying the countryside. It was a pleasant but tiring time for them, and they got back with a few days to rest up before Mike finally had to go back to the department and start working again. When he did go back, he was assigned to duties that took him as far away from his previous work as possible. It was well known that there was a contract out on his head and the police didn't want him where it could be collected.

16

Darlene finally told Dolly that she was expecting again, which brought tears to Dolly's eyes. She was watching her daughter develop a family and couldn't help getting emotional. She had never dared to hope that she would be so hands-on in the development and available to help her daughter in times of need.

Victoria was now over two years old and getting around chasing the ducks, wading in the pond, and generally keeping Darlene or Dolly or both on their toes. She was turning into a cute little girl with curly blond hair and a natural smile. Victoria adored her father and took every opportunity to climb on his lap and sit there in triumph. Mike came to the farm as often as possible but was using one of the bedrooms in the house during the week. It was thought that the danger to him and his family was decreasing, but no chances were taken. Three of the commandos remained at the house and it was deemed a safe area.

Mike worked behind a desk in the station with no input on the investigation that had so nearly cost him his life on at least two occasions. Darlene's pregnancy began to show and she started taking things easy as her mother took over more of the housework at the farm. It was decided that Darlene would move back into town just before the baby was born, and that Dolly would go along to take care of things for the first few weeks. Fred had to stay and take care of the horses, which he didn't mind.

The baby came in August. Darlene was again in the hospital for scarcely two days before she was released to go home. The new baby girl weighed in at ten pounds three ounces. Mike took the news very well, considering that he had desperately wanted the baby to be male. He continued to work from eight a.m. to five p.m. Monday through Friday with no nights or weekends on his schedule. He didn't know how long such a position would last, but he intended to enjoy it with his family while he could. Dolly left after a few days because Darlene was completely capable of taking care of herself.

Mike drove her out to the farm in the new van and then came back to spend a quiet evening with his wife.

Another police officer was gunned down by the criminals that had attacked Mike. The officer suffered a spinal injury from gunshot wounds and was diagnosed as paraplegic. There was suddenly a strong argument for having Mike return to his former duties. Unfortunately, he had no say in the matter and had to do what the brass decided. They said that he was the best officer that they had for that job. When Mike told Darlene that starting the following Monday, he would be back on nights and weekends putting himself in a position to get killed, she wasn't the least bit impressed. She said that perhaps it was time that he thought about some other line of work. The problem was of course, that he knew police work and nothing else. If he tried to switch careers, he would have to start at the bottom.

The only other alternative would be for Darlene to return to work and Mike to become a full-time stay-at-home father. Darlene wouldn't make as much money as he did but at least it would be much more likely that they'd both stay alive. Mike wasn't very impressed with her idea. Besides, they couldn't really stand a twenty thousand per year reduction in household income.

The final decision was for Mike to go back to his normal duties with Darlene staying home to care for the little ones. She now had little Joanie to accompany Victoria in the double stroller that she pushed along the walkways. Like Victoria, Joanie was going to be a blond girl with big blue eyes that were almost like large berries of the same name. Darlene knew that she was going to spend sleepless nights while her husband was involved in high-risk police work but there didn't seem to be an immediate solution to the problem. To make matters worse, almost as soon as Mike started back working nights carrying a machine gun, he began receiving threatening faxes at work and threatening letters at home. Darlene didn't know how long she was going to be able to take it.

It was decided that she wasn't going to hide this time. No running to the farm to live with her mother. Instead she brought the rifles into the city and mounted them around the house out of the children's reach. She also bought a few more handguns and planted them discreetly around the house. Now, she wore her holster everywhere and occasionally practiced drawing her gun, much to the consternation of whoever saw her. Darlene became indifferent; she was tired of living like a criminal.

Sometimes during the night, cars seemed to drive by the house slowly or pull into the driveway. She'd think that Mike was coming home until the car suddenly took off again. It was a recurring event. She was almost afraid to go shopping but refused to give in to the harassment. She regularly took her children in the van to shop for groceries and eventually began to feel that she was going to be left alone. Once she heard gunfire around her house and a few minutes later Mike got home. He said that if there had been gunfire it wasn't related to him, but Darlene wasn't so sure. She started to notice gray hairs although she wasn't yet thirty years old: her mother hardly had any gray and she was past fifty.

Darlene used every trick in the book to lure her friends to her house to spend the night with her. She had a police officer's wife or an off-duty nurse staying with her as often as possible. Part of this was for company but she also reasoned that if she cut loose and killed somebody again, she wanted a reliable witness. She was getting so edgy that killing would be a relief to her. At least, that's how she felt most of the time.

Mike even wore a bulletproof vest to church on Sundays. He never went anywhere without one on. The department had arranged for him to be at home to attend with his wife and children every Sunday because just about any other time he had no idea when he'd be home. When he was, he played with his two little girls constantly so that they would know their father and love him.

Darlene would sit happily and watch him on the floor playing with the girls. When he was home, they snuggled and hugged each other as if every minute together was a precious piece of time that could be snatched away by the criminals' bullets. Each time Mike had to leave for work, Darlene braced herself for him not coming home again. The department was paying for a major life insurance policy, so at least they didn't have to pay the premium for that. Still, it was small comfort to either of them.

Mike occasionally told Darlene what his night's work had been like. He often was involved in raids and takedowns where a number of men were arrested. Sometimes shots were fired, and two more police officers had been hurt since the one who had become a paraplegic.

Later on, Darlene said that it was inevitable, simply a matter of time. That was when she and other members of the force were sitting discussing the situation. When it happened and immediately afterward though, she was hardly able to speak at all, she was so angry.

It happened one day after she had finished doing the day's grocery shopping. Her van was loaded up and she was just about to head home. She pulled out on to the roadway when a car came up beside her on the left side, and the passenger shoved a shotgun towards her window and pulled the trigger. Darlene slammed on her brakes, which meant the shot went across in front of her instead of through her. She also stopped her vehicle, jumped out, and fired two shots at the fleeing car. One bullet got a tire, causing the vehicle to swerve and hit a fire hydrant. A tower of water spewed into the air. The car came to a stop right on top of the hydrant and she fired a second shot, which took off part of the driver's head. Then she ran to the side of the car and told the passenger to get out and lie on the ground before she blew him away too. He did, eyes bulging with fright and hands in the air. Someone came running up, and Darlene told them to call the police.

"I thought that you were the police!" the woman said.

"Use my cell phone if you don't have one. Call 911 and hurry. I can't hold this bastard here forever." The woman got her phone out and called, and in a few minutes a patrol car showed up. The driver jumped out and pointed his gun at Darlene ordering her to drop her weapon. She lowered it and told the man who she was. He didn't flinch, simply yelled at her to drop her gun again, and she did so. He then turned to the man on the ground and covered him as Frank showed up along with another officer. They took control of the situation and relieved the patrolman of the criminal on the ground. He still had his gun and pointed it at Darlene again. Frank told him that she was one of them, which made the cop look questioningly at him before putting his gun away. She certainly didn't look like she was one of them but Frank was the senior officer. Darlene went back to her car to check on her two children. They were sitting in their car seats wide-eyed and quiet. She smiled at them, smoothed the hair across their foreheads and went back to Frank.

Quickly, she explained the situation and showed him her car's obliterated side window. He stood looking grimly at it, knowing what this meant; half an hour later he put in a call for Mike, just as the ambulances and fire trucks were leaving, Mike showed up, gave Darlene a bear hug, then got the details from her and Frank. He too looked grim. They had easily identified the dead man and knew that Darlene was definitely on the criminal organization's hit list.

Mike escorted Darlene home by following her in an unmarked police car. Frank followed both of them once the scene was completely cleaned up and the hydrant shut off. They sat in Mike and Darlene's kitchen having coffee and talking over the event.

"That's another notch you can put on that gun of yours." Mike said with a bit of a smile. "You should take over my job. You do more damage to the organization than anyone else." Darlene giggled nervously. She didn't want to let on how good it felt to get some of her own back against the people that were making her husband's and family's life miserable. It felt good and she wanted more of it.

Growing up in Siberia she had never handled a gun, not even seen any except the ones that the soldiers carried, and she'd certainly never gotten a close look at those. When Mike had first introduced her to a handgun, she had found it repulsive and frightening.

However, once he had coaxed her to learn how to use the weapon, she had begun to enjoy it and went back for more practice by herself. Then, when the time came for her to protect herself, she had done so with relish. She had found it exhilarating, and sometimes asked herself why. She never did figure out how or why she felt better after dropping some piece of scum, she just did. She enjoyed it.

The officers sat in her living room trying to figure out how they were going to protect her from future assaults. As she didn't intend to run and hide, there was little they could do unless they provided her with an escort when she went out. That was unfeasible because of the costs. She smiled as she told Mike that now he could worry about her for a change. Eventually, both Frank and Mike had to resume their work. After making sure that Darlene was fine and was at no risk from going into shock, they left. She called her mother and told her some of what had happened, leaving out the worst parts.

Her mother of course was mortified, especially when Darlene told her that one of the culprits was dead. Darlene just laughed, then changed the subject, saying that she was planning to have a party for Mike's thirty-sixth birthday, and that Dolly and Fred should come on in. They had chased down an old Ford truck which Fred had fixed up and now drove. It was green with white on the sides and a very sturdy vehicle for its age.

Mike was of course driving Darlene's Mercedes to work so that she could use the van to haul the children and groceries around. When she took the van in to have the window repaired and told the attendant that the window had been shot out, she smiled inwardly at the look she got from him. That's the way life was right now. A war was going on, and she was now smack in the middle of it.

17

Needless to say, security measures were tightened up around the Strong's home. Everything was checked over, new more sophisticated alarm systems were put in place, and there wasa regular drive-by done by the police. They drove by every few hours on a seemingly haphazard basis so that no one could predict when they would appear. They would knock on the door during that period when Darlene could be expected to be up. She welcomed the police presence and always invited them to stop for coffee. Sometimes they accepted. Patrolmen were getting to know her and the one who had held a gun on her now laughed with embarrassment every time he saw her. She made it clear though that she didn't hold it against him.

For the next few months, things were quiet. Nobody bothered Darlene, at least not that she knew about. She said that she wouldn't always know if someone was following her, just if they made a move on her, and by that time she'd be in it up to her ears again. But she didn't sound like she was afraid of that happening.

One afternoon when Mike was just about to leave for work, he received what sounded like a frantic phone call from the station. They said how glad they were to have reached him and then told him not to go anywhere near his vehicles until further notice. He also wasn't to come to work until someone came to pick him up. He had no idea what was going on but shortly a truck full of technicians arrived and began checking his vehicles over. They found nothing wrong with the van but the Mercedes had a bomb wired to the ignition and that, of course, was the vehicle he would have driven to work. Except he wouldn't have made it out of the driveway.

He was picked up by Frank, in an unmarked police car: the department decided that for the foreseeable future, he would be driven to and from work. His vehicles would be checked twice a day for bombs. Darlene sat watching as the world closed in around her again. Would they ever even have a semblance of normal life again? That was the question that ran through her mind.

One day shortly after this, a woman from the department phoned to make an appointment with Darlene. She came out, had a coffee while they got acquainted and talked about the children, then got started. She had brought with her a small suitcase of papers and spread some of them on the kitchen table. Then she began teaching Darlene all about bombs, land mines and booby traps. She spent three hours with Darlene and made a future appointment to continue the briefings until Darlene knew everything that she would need to know about protecting herself and her family. She was taught how to recognize a letter bomb and what to do if a strange package arrived on her doorstep. She was taught how to examine the vehicles for attached bombs before she got into them and how to be aware of booby traps that might detonate even before she got in the vehicle. Darlene spent hours rehearsing the procedures until they became automatic. The lady, whose name was Beth, was skilled at her work, and in no time she and Darlene were buddies. Beth was originally from the military and had been trained as an engineer. She was knowledgeable about land mines that were made to look like children's toys, deadly devices that could be placed where Darlene's children might pick them up. Darlene could hardly believe what she was learning. She looked at the devices in horror and imagined Victoria finding such a thing on the lawn Beth normally taught Special Forces police officers how to protect themselves when on a mission. Mike had described his family's situation and without too much difficulty convinced her to spend these few sessions with Darlene so that she could keep their children safe. He hoped that she'd never need to use the knowledge. Mike had been a student of Beth's many years ago and attended regular refresher sessions. He could have passed on to Darlene the learning he had acquired but chose instead to have Beth do it because she was an expert, and

Darlene would take it more seriously. Darlene took the information more seriously. Darlene didn't miss a detail.

She had now found herself a very nice young babysitter named Lisa, who was a delight with both Victoria and Joanie. She would later recount that she had no idea how she found Lisa, who seemed to have just popped up. Actually she met Lisa at the supermarket one day, and a conversation had started, an innocuous conversation that led to Darlene saying that she'd be interested in having Lisa take care of her children once in a while. Then she discussed it with Mike before agreeing to try Lisa with the children.

Lisa was seventeen years old but mature for her age as well as very friendly and knowledgeable. Darlene left her with the children for just a few hours the first time, and then the sessions grew longer. She had Lisa sit for her about once a week at the start.

One day when Mike came by the house after Lisa had just left, Darlene had the brilliant idea of taking Lisa's fingerprints off a glass and running them through the system. Mike willingly obliged. The next time that Lisa was going to babysit, Mike called and told Darlene to treat her a little coldly to give her the idea that they were on to her. Then he told Darlene that she wasn't the seventeen she had claimed, she was twenty-seven. She was also the girlfriend of one of their prime suspects. Mike said that they wanted to catch her in the act if possible and wanted to frighten her into action.

When Lisa got to the house, Darlene snapped at her and said that it would probably be the last time she'd sit for them. She said that she hadn't checked Lisa out properly but was intending to do it that day. She didn't explain how.

Mike had gotten a court order to tap his own telephone, so it was legal and admissible as evidence. No sooner did Darlene leave than Lisa called her boyfriend. She didn't get him on the line but talked to one of his cohorts, telling him that they'd better move right away if they wanted to kidnap the children. Lisa spoke urgently, saying she was being processed by the police and that she'd be in deep trouble as soon as they found out about the connections to her boyfriend. The listener agreed and arranged to come by in half an hour.

"You have to come right away!" screamed Lisa. "This is desperate here. She is going to be back soon, and I want to be gone before that bitch comes back!" Mike looked grim as he sat in a van listening in a few hundred yards away. He radioed his officers and they got into position. They wanted to catch as many as possible in the net that they were casting. Meanwhile, Lisa got the children ready, packing the little one in a car seat and getting Victoria dressed for traveling.

They watched as an old red van very familiar to Mike pulled into his driveway. Darlene was also sitting in the listening post vehicle and had heard everything. She was furious that her children were in the hands of kidnappers who intended to spirit them away somewhere, and her fists clenched when she heard Lisa refer to her as "that bitch". The police stealthily got themselves into position so that no one could get off the property in any direction.

A short stocky very grubby man of about forty brought Joanie out and placed her in the red van. Then he went back and got Victoria. He urged her to get in the van also, but she refused saying loudly that she wasn't going anywhere with him. Mike grinned at his spunky young daughter but wished that she'd co-operate so that they could get on with it. The man pulled a knife out of his trousers and tried to force Victoria into the van. The little girl fought with him, but Lisa quickly came out and coaxed her into the van.

Lisa and the man were beside the van, just about to get in when they were swarmed by police. They didn't have time to get the children to use as shields or hostages. Before they knew what had hit them, they were face down on the driveway.

When they were safely inside a police car Darlene snatched the girls from the van, then stood outside the squad car glaring at the girl who had intended to steal her children.

Lisa glared back defiantly. Mike and the officers gave the van a once over and then decided to take it to the lab for a full analysis. It had obvious bloodstains in it, and one of the police dogs began barking like crazy. No doubt there were drugs on board as well.

Darlene got her children back into the house and calmed them down. She told Victoria what a brave girl she was and that she had been right not to want to go with the man. She told them both that she and Daddy had been watching and would never let anything bad happen to them. When she got them calmed down and playing, she put the coffee pot on in case any of the officers intended to hang around. None did but she gratefully sat down to enjoy a cup herself, deeply relieved that the episode had ended well but wondering what might come to plague them next.

18

That September, Victoria began going to kindergarten. Darlene drove her to the half-day session each day and picked her up again when it was over. The teacher was discreetly drilled onthe necessity of caution concerning the little girl and advised that there was the possibility that someone might attempt to harm her. A number of safety precautions were put in place with the agreement that Victoria would be watched over all the time and not allowed to be alone anywhere.

Mike was thrilled at how his daughter was growing up. He bragged to everybody about how she stood up for herself against a dangerous kidnapper, and he visited her at daycare sometimes while he was in uniform. He was proud of Victoria and used every opportunity to make her proud of her father too. He also spent as much time with Joanie. He loved both his children and vowed that the next time Darlene found a babysitter, the first thing that they would do was run her through the system. Fingerprinting and a thorough background check were mandatory before anyone began the job. He knew that getting a sitter was important so that Darlene could get away occasionally from the housework. She had a large network of friends whom she wanted to visit and spend time with. What Mike didn't know and what would have caused some discussion was that Darlene wanted to return to work. She was planning on it but had yet to announce it to Mike. She was intending to return to work once Joanie began attending kindergarten.

Mike and Darlene had a very close relationship. Her only complaint was that he was away from home too much. He worked long hours and too many days in a row before he got a break. The only exception was that he was able to attend the morning service at church every Sunday. Then he often had to go right back to work after having lunch with his wife and children. Sometimes he was in uniform, sometimes not. His daughters were used to seeing him in uniform and were used to being around police officers in a way that most children were not.

Darlene had both her children attending Sunday school, getting formal teaching in things that were right. As the children grew older, they became more mature and knowledgeable about many things. They were getting a well-rounded education.

Darlene had never severed her relationship with the friends she had made as a nurse and saw as many of them as she could as often as possible. She knew that having accomplished the feat of having a family, it was getting to be time to go back to the work she loved. It would mean having a full time housekeeper and that's what she was planning to do. The question was where would she find such a person? She had numerous feelers out but hadn't received so much as a nibble so far.

Dolly was making friends too. She and Fred drove the old truck he had bought into the city occasionally to visit with other Russian immigrants. They were quite surprised to find a small but tightly-knit community of Russian people in the area. Dolly knew that Darlene was trying to find a housekeeper and told her daughter that she had to tell her husband sometime; sooner was better. Darlene, however, was a bit nervous about how Mike would react to the suggestion. While she fretted over this dilemma, she kept looking for a lady who could fill her requirements.

Time passed very slowly for Darlene, who already had a full complement of new uniforms waiting to be used. It passed like a prairie wind for Mike as he watched his daughters growing up before his eyes. Joanie was set to begin kindergarten as soon as she turned four. At the same time, Victoria would enroll in grade one and Darlene would be free at last to return to work. Dolly invited Darlene to an afternoon tea one day with several other women that were her friends and introduced Darlene to a lady referred to as Mrs. Isaacs. She spoke English but just barely, and Darlene paid little attention to her. Long afterwards when Dolly was at Darlene's, Dolly asked her what she thought of Mrs. Isaacs.

"She's nice I suppose. Why?"

"She wants to be your housekeeper. Did she make any impression on you?"

"Well, I'll have to think about it some. Tell me all you know about her."

So, Dolly shared what she knew. Mrs. Isaacs and her husband had come over from Russia nine years ago, but her husband had recently passed away. She was in her late forties and alone now and was looking for a live-in position where she could take care of the children and the house. She had a driver's license plus her own little car if needed. She could provide references, of whom Dolly would be one. Dolly had now known her for three years. She spoke passable English as well as her native Russian. Finally, she was willing to have any kind of check on her past that was required.

It had really become time now to discuss the situation with Mike. One night when Mike got home, Darlene got up out of bed and invited him to sit and have a beer with her before he turned in. It wasn't an unusual gesture; she did it occasionally. She almost always got up when he came home, but most of the time they had a cup of tea, hot chocolate, or coffee. Both could sleep easily after drinking coffee so that wasn't a problem. It was when Darlene had something she wanted to talk over with Mike that they'd have a beer. Even knowing this, he was in no way prepared for what she wanted to discuss.

"I've been thinking about going back to being a nurse now that Joanie is starting kindergarten." Mike looked at her. She hastily added, "There's no sense in me just sitting here waiting for the kids to come home. I want to do something. Something worthwhile."

She explained about the housekeeper, about how it would all work and described every advantage to the situation that she could think of. When she was finished she took a sip of beer and waited. Mike had questions, lots of them, but he knew that when his wife had made her mind up about something, it was best to just let her have her way. Mike sat thinking about the ramifications of his wife's proposal. True, a housekeeper could drive the kids just as easily as Darlene and could take care of the house. It wasn't that they needed the money, both of them knew that. It was that Darlene wanted to be active, to be involved in life just like Mike. Both of them knew that, too. Darlene wanted to go for lunch with her friends while she was at work. Her husband was on the cutting edge in his profession and she wanted to be in hers. He couldn't think of a suitable argument to stop her from doing what she wanted.

So she got two more beers while they worked out the schedule. She described Mrs. Isaacs and said that she was willing to come to the police department for a thorough background check. Reaching out she took Mike's hand as they thought about a new and different era of their lives. They had children now, children who had graduated to that place in life where they would start the formal learning process. They looked at each other with almost worshipful love, as they realized that they were growing older with their children.

Both the children were excellent swimmers and enjoyed going to the lake. Both grew up around the horses and loved horseback riding. When Victoria began going to grade school, she soon became popular by having her father come to the school in uniform so that the other children could ask him questions about his work.

Around the station Mike was teased about becoming an old softie, but during a takedown he was cold steel all the time. He was still heavily involved in interfering with gangs and gang warfare. He did lots of plain-clothes work, undercover work and night shifts. While he occasionally was in uniform, he was far enough up the ladder that he could wear just about anything and did. He was anything but a nine-to-five daytime cop. If he worked days at all, he began at 6:30 a.m. or some time like that. He would probably work until seven or eight in the evening if he was lucky. Sometimes he started out to work a day shift and was gone for eighteen to twenty- four hours.

Occasionally, he would be around the house for the whole day or even a couple of days. That was when his daughters enjoyed getting to know him all over again, and his wife snuggled with him on the sofa. Theirs was in no way an ordinary life. It wasn't meant to be, they didn't try to make it ordinary, and they just accepted what came along unless it was threatening. Then they gathered their forces and fought back with every weapon at their disposal. Fortunately, they had weapons in their arsenal that other people couldn't even begin to imagine.

Now, with his daughters attending their respective schools, quality time was more precious than ever before. If they got to the lake or to the farm, the activity was intense and very enjoyable. There were now four horses that the Strong's could use for riding, and they often went as a group across the countryside. There were also two canoes, which allowed the whole family to enjoy the lake together.

Astoundingly, there didn't seem to be any concerted effort to harm Darlene or the girls for a long time. The criminals who had tried were either in jail or had made other plans.

Too many had died or gotten arrested while tampering with Mrs. Strong and her family. In fact, Darlene had something of a reputation around the police department as being someone not to be fooled with.

To almost no one's surprise, Victoria and Joanie were very popular at school and instrumental in developing a rapport between police officers and children. Friends who came over to the Strongs' house to play often found themselves surrounded by uniformed officers when Mike was hosting a session of some kind. He often had a group of officers meet with him at his home to plan strategies or attacks. He had the meetings at the house so that he could check in and make sure everything was going smoothly.

Darlene, as planned, was back at work in the hospital. The head nurse was someone new, but just about everyone else was the same apart from having aged. She fit in perfectly and was soon back to working the same basic shifts as her husband. Sometimes they would get home at the same time in the morning. She loved the night shifts and worked it out with Mrs. Isaacs so that she could indulge herself, and the housekeeper would fill in while she was at work. This gave Mrs. Isaacs some time off during the day when Darlene was at home. Also, while Mrs. Isaacs had to be on call during the night, she could sleep if everything was well. Darlene was not a demanding boss. She and Mrs. Isaacs worked out a plan that benefited both of them.

One evening at about 8 p.m. Darlene was sitting with two other nurses as they had their supper. She looked around at the cafeteria, which was filled with hospital staff, and glowed. She loved being back at work. She loved wearing her clean white uniform and being accepted as a professional. Elsie, a new staff member, was talking about having found a room in a house near the hospital, and suddenly Darlene realized that Elsie was talking about her very own house. She giggled. They looked at her questioningly.

"Is May still living in that house?"

"Yes of course she is. Do you know her?"

"Yes I do. She sends me the rent check for the house regular as clock work."

"What? I don't understand." Elsie looked at her.

"You're moving into my house. I'm glad you found a place.

That's what it's there for."

Elsie was surprised and then got Darlene to tell the story of how she had come to own the house in the first place. Darlene emphasized that the house was strictly for nurses, and that it had now been in operation for several years. Elsie found it hard to believe that she was sitting right next to someone who must be fairly well off, but she hid her thoughts, merely asking Darlene why she was working at all. Darlene shrugged and replied that she wanted to do something useful. She then told about having two beautiful children, a husband who was a police officer, and much more.

"Mike… I know him. He comes in here sometimes to check on somebody that we've got on the ward. He usually comes in with a guy called Frank."

That started a whole new conversation as Darlene related how much she enjoyed the company of Frank and Wanda. Wanda had transferred to another floor and worked mostly days now. They were still talking animatedly when it was time to go back up to the wards.

Darlene hadn't seen May in quite a while. She received the rent regularly and had no reason to seek her out. Darlene was not involved in who would be sublet the house; she had simply told May that the place was for nurses who wanted to live near the hospital, but it was May who had to keep the house full. If she decided to rent to nuns or soldiers, then that was her business. Darlene was glad to hear from Elsie that May was continuing to rent to nurses.

Darlene still carried her little gun with her everywhere. She had been burned too many times to think that she would ever go anywhere without it. Elsie as well as many other nurses who hadn't been working there at the time had nonetheless heard about Darlene's shoot-out on the hospital steps. The story was often told so that nurses would exercise the utmost caution when leaving the hospital in the early morning or after dark. The policy of having someone from security walk nurses to their cars or to the bus stop was fully in place and rigorously followed.

Soon after she returned to work, nurses that Darlene had never seen in her life began stopping her or seeking her out to discuss security measures and her actions when attacked. One day the hospital asked Darlene if she would host a seminar on safety measures at which nurses could learn about how to defend themselves if attacked. She agreed to do it and soon became something of a celebrity at the hospital.

Darlene told the other nurses during the seminar that she carried a gun with her at all times and explained how they might do the same. She related how she had initially found guns to be repulsive until she began learning how to shoot, but she did not tell them how many times she had used a gun against another person. She did emphasize that everyone should take lessons on how to defend themselves if attacked and also on how to reduce the risk of such attacks.

The only place that Darlene didn't keep her gun on her person was at home. It hung in the holster on a high peg in the bedroom. Both her children had been introduced to the various weapons in the house and told that they were never to touch them. The little girls were obedient.

Mrs. Isaacs had been working for the Strong's for almost a year when things went terribly wrong. Darlene was in the shower when her husband phoned. Mrs. Isaacs called Darlene and asked if she wanted to take it or have him call back. Wrapping herself in a bright red bathrobe, she said that she'd take the call.

"Hi, honey. What's on your mind?"

"We have just gotten some information about Mrs. Isaacs that might interest you. Before she was married in Russia, her name was Florence Goldbaum. She is the daughter of Jacob Goldbaum. Her father was a diamond merchant who was murdered in your home town, Petronovak." There was a stunned silence on the phone as Darlene digested this information.

"Hello…are you there?"

Yes, darling I'm here. Thank you for telling me, but it could have waited until you came home. It isn't important."

"It isn't? I thought that you'd be interested. OK, I'll see you tonight."

Darlene hung up the phone slowly. Her mind was whirling and she could hardly take in what Mike had told her. She grasped the back of a chair to steady herself, then turned to look at Mrs. Isaacs, and a look of horror appeared on her face.

Mrs. Isaacs was holding Darlene's gun and pointing it at her belly.

"Mrs. Isaacs, put that thing down and let's talk about this."

"What's to talk about? Now you know all about me and I know all about you. I came here to find you. I didn't know what I'd do if I found you, but now I'm going to turn you over to the police, who will send you back to Russia for questioning. The district police have ways of finding out the truth. STAND STILL!"

Darlene had been inching towards a desk that had a small caliber gun in one of the drawers. She was now beside the desk and could do as she was ordered. She froze, only her fingers continued to move ever so slightly. She couldn't remember which drawer the gun was in. She would have to make her first move a good one.

Mrs. Isaacs was dialing the telephone when Darlene dived for the floor and opened first one and then all of the drawers spilling the contents out onto the floor. She grabbed the black automatic as Mrs. Isaacs fired at her and missed. Darlene didn't miss: the bullet hit Mrs. Isaacs in the stomach. The woman screamed Russian swear words at Darlene as she fell to the floor clutching her abdomen. The wound wasn't a bad one, superficial but enough to slow the Russian woman down.

Darlene went over and kicked the gun away from where it had fallen, out of Mrs. Isaacs' reach. Then she stood looking down at the woman as she hung up the telephone.

"You think that you know me? You don't know anything. Nada! Nada! She aimed her little black automatic and shot Mrs. Isaacs squarely in the head. Then she put the gun down and called the police.

"Hello…this is an emergency. I just killed someone in our house. Could you put me through to Mike Strong? Please…this is his wife Darlene." She heard the officer gasp, and then she had to wait until Mike came on the phone.

"Hi, hon…what's up?"

"When you called me, Mrs. Isaacs was apparently listening in on our conversation. When I got off the phone she was pointing my own gun at me and threatening to kill me. She had this stupid idea that I killed her father and intended to get revenge."

"Well, you obviously aren't dead, so what happened?"

"I got another gun put of the desk drawer. I am afraid she won't make it, I think she's dead."

"Did she actually try to kill you?"

"Yes she shot at me....I shot back and wounded her. She shot at me again, and I think that I killed her. Can you come home, darling?....I need you."

Mike sighed heavily, "I'll be right there with a crew to clean up.

See you in five minutes."

Darlene hung up the phone. Then she took her regular gun off the floor very carefully and, without leaving any prints on it, fired it again into the wall where she had been standing. Then she placed the gun near Mrs. Isaac's hand and went into the kitchen to put the coffee pot on.

The police came. Mike walked in looking very grim. There was a photographer, a couple of ambulance attendants, a coroner and several others. Darlene sat looking dejected and shaken. Mike put his arm around her to comfort her while he surveyed the scene in the front room. He got Darlene to explain where she had been standing.

She had to show where Mrs. Isaacs had been standing and the bullet holes in the wall. Mike picked up Darlene's gun gingerly and checked the loads. It had been fired twice. There were two bullet holes in the wall. Darlene's story seemed to fit, but he wondered what had really happened and whether or not he should try to find out.

By this time in his life, Mike Strong loved Darlene so much that even if she had committed outright murder, he would have protected her. She was the mother of his two beautiful daughters and a loyal, faithful wife. He thought often about the dark side of her but couldn't believe that she was anything but what she appeared to be.

He knew that he could make an official investigation into certain little things that remained unanswered questions, but he wouldn't. By this time in their marriage, he'd gone over the issue with himself a thousand times. He just wanted to love her and have her love him forever. He wanted his children to grow up with both a mother and a father. It was an uphill struggle because he was always in danger himself. And it irritated him that every time he turned around his wife was put in a situation of killing someone and upsetting the already delicate balance of their family life. But every marriage had its challenges, he supposed.

While the other officers worked, he sat with Darlene drinking a coffee while his mind was on what had happened in their front room. Darlene was supposed to go to work in a while. What were they going to do with the children now? When he asked her that, she shrugged and told him that he had put in almost a full day's work. Why didn't he just stay here and pick up the kids from their school while she went to work? As had happened after previous incidents, she seemed so cold and removed from what she had done. He couldn't understand it. She wasn't as upset as she ought to be, and she even wanted to go to work.

It was Darlene's inclination to call her mother to come and take care of the children for a few days until they could find another housekeeper. Mike wanted Darlene to stay home from work until they found somebody, but she replied that she'd be damned if she was going to return to being a housewife and nothing else just because the house keeper had tried to kill her. While Darlene called her mother, Mike sat sipping his coffee and seething.

After the body was removed, after all the officers had left, Mike and Darlene came as close to having a fight as they ever had. Mike thought that Darlene should stay home with the children. Darlene explained to him that if she sat around all evening stewing about what had happened, she'd be more of a mess. Work would take her mind off the incident. She said that perhaps in a few days she'd arrange to stay at home for a while, but right now, she was going to work. Mike knew that his little Muscovite was stubborn, bull-headed and determined. He knew it, but he nonetheless resented it. She was the stronger one of the two in the marriage, which was fine most of the time but in cases such as this, it became a source of extreme displeasure.

So Mike ended up calling in and reporting that there had been trouble at his house, and he had to remain there. When it was time for school to end, he went to pick up both Victoria and Joanie. With the evening now free to be spent with his children, he forgot about Darlene and the troubles as he prepared a meal for the three of them.

Darlene meanwhile was on edge and not at all her happy, congenial self. As she worked, she wondered about the effect that Mrs. Isaacs' demise would have on their marriage. It was too bad that she'd had to kill the woman, but letting her live would have been disastrous. She went about with a grim look on her face and silently cursed the day she'd ever set eyes on that Russian woman. When she finished her shift and got home, she quietly got into bed and curled up alongside Mike. He woke up, and they lay talking for a few minutes about things. He was in a better mood and when she finally got to sleep, she felt a lot better.

They got up in the morning to find Dolly banging on the front door. She came in like a whirlwind demanding to know what had happened to Mrs. Isaacs. Mike's face tightened and he looked to his wife and said, "Go ahead Darlene, tell her what happened to Mrs. Isaacs. Darlene also looked grim as she struggled to find words for her mother. She looked helplessly at Mike, who relented and came over to put his arm around her. He told Dolly that Mrs. Isaacs was dead, that she had been killed while attempting to shoot Darlene with her own gun. When Dolly was finally able to speak, she railed about the existence of guns in the house at all pointing out that the situation would never have happened if there had been no guns around in the first place. Having gotten this off her chest, she calmed down and gave Darlene a comforting hug.

Mike asked Darlene what her shift at the hospital had been like, and Darlene replied that it would have been better if she had stayed away. "You were right, Mike, I should have stayed home. There was no sense in my venting my anger on my patients and colleagues, and that was what I was doing. I told the head nurse that I was having problems, and she said that she'd understand if I took a few days off to get things straightened out. The trouble is, I have no idea where to find another housekeeper."

Dolly had just come back in from dropping the children off at school. After spending even that brief time with the girls, she was bright and cheerful despite the grim atmosphere that prevailed. She jumped in with the remark that she knew of another woman who might be interested, but she certainly didn't want Darlene to shoot this one too. Darlene laughed rudely as she looked at her mother to see if she was serious. She was.

Mike was supposed to have gone to work but had called in with an excuse. The three of them sat around the kitchen table sipping coffee and talking things over. The Strongs began exploring every avenue to find themselves a housekeeper. They found an elite agency and indicated that they were looking for a woman that could work all shifts, and that they preferred one who could live there. This request brought a woman by the name of Audrey Prince to their house. She was a recent immigrant from Wales and spoke with a very distinct accent. She claimed that she was experienced at doing the kind of work required and was looking for a live-in position. Mike and Darlene looked at each other. The agency had assured them that they screened all of their candidates very thoroughly. They nodded and the three of them started discussing the details of the position.

Audrey had her own car, which freed up Darlene's. When she was told that an in-depth police check would be done on her background, she giggled and said, "They do that to everybody everywhere on the British Isles because of criminals and terrorists. It's no big deal."

Mike reached into his briefcase and produced a blank fingerprint form, an inkpad and a roller. He covered the inkpad with black ink and then made a very professional copy of Audrey's fingerprints right there on the kitchen table. Audrey's eyes grew large as she witnessed the police officer in action. It was driven home to her that Mike led a fairly dangerous life, and that she was to exercise the utmost caution at all times.

The home had a sophisticated alarm system that Audrey would have to learn. She was told that there were a number of guns on the premises at all times. She didn't particularly like that but said she could stand it as long as they weren't lying around carelessly. She was told that it would take a few days before the background check was complete, and at that time she'd be notified as to whether or not she could have the position.

After supplying all required information and documents, Audrey left. Mike looked at Darlene hopefully. Perhaps they had found the new housekeeper.

As the days went by, Mike got into a deep and disturbing depression. He didn't like the fact that Mrs. Isaacs had been killed. He had liked her, grown fond of her and thought that she was "nice." She had asked a few indiscreet questions of him, and he had thought nothing of it. Now, in hindsight, one could believe that she was searching for proof and had an ulterior motive for asking the questions besides being there at all. She had certainly gotten herself into a bad spot, but she didn't deserve to die because of it. His feelings about the situation got worse when a ballistics report indicated that she had probably been murdered rather than shot in self-defense.

With determination and sorrow, Mike went to a few different pawnbrokers asking about diamonds. He didn't have to go very far before he found out exactly what he knew but didn't want to hear. Yes, a young woman had brought in a bunch of diamonds. Forty- two in all, diamonds of superior quality and worth. Mike couldn't see them, they were scattered around the globe by now, but he got dates, times, and description of the woman. It was Darlene. He now knew that she had murdered the diamond merchant; it was beyond doubt.

He loved his little Muscovite dearly, but he had to face that she had murdered at least once and probably twice. He was a police officer, and could no longer turn his back on the truth. The police department wanted to prosecute his wife for the murder of Mrs.

Isaacs. He told the district attorney that he'd take care of it. Then he contacted the Russian Embassy and told them that he had proof that the murderer of Jacob Goldbaum was in the city. It took a few days before some Russian police officers contacted Mike while he was at work. He took them to the pawnshop first and then told them where they could find Darlene. She was taken into custody by local officers while she was at work. At the station, she was told that she was charged with the murder of Jacob Goldbaum, and Russian police officers were going to transport her back to her Russian homeland. Mike was not anywhere around and stayed clear of the whole proceeding.

That night, he went to visit her in her cell and said that the Russian police knew about the diamonds. He said that he loved her, but that she would have been charged with the murder of Mrs. Isaacs if she had remained in Newark. He was crying as he told her that there was nothing that he could do to help her out of this terrible predicament.

The next person to come to see her was her mother. Dolly sobbed for her daughter, knowing that they would probably never see each other again. They sat silently contemplating the future. Dolly cried again and held her only daughter tightly.

Darlene didn't cry. She had no idea how things could have taken such a turn for the worse. In her wildest imagination she never considered that Mike had any thing to do with her being arrested. She sat in the cell cold as steel, contemplating life in a Russian prison. But she didn't cry.

Neither she nor Mike had any idea what might happen to her holdings in the U.S., so she willingly transferred everything into his name through a lawyer before she left the country. It was for their children's sake she told Mike. She insisted that someday she'd see her children again. Truthfully, she had no idea how rough being in a Russian prison would be, or how long she would be in one.

Mike went with her to the airport. He gave her one final kiss good-bye before she was taken aboard the plane, and his heart cried out for strength as he watched her go. He knew that he could never have continued to work as a police officer if he hadn't finally done the right thing. He knew also that watching her walk down the long hallway to the plane would be the very last time that he'd ever see his little Muscovite.

19

By the time the plane left Heathrow, Darlene was desperate. She knew she wouldn't last in a Russian prison. Her escorts treated her roughly, like some kind of farm animal. One pawed her and used every opportunity to maul her breasts. She knew that once she got to Russia, worse was in store.

The two uniformed soldiers bringing her back to Russia were becoming but drab. Their clothes were wrinkled and threadbare: even the higher-ups in the Russian military couldn't get the good stuff. These two had spent the previous evening carousing despite knowing that they were flying early the next day. Hung-over, exhausted, and hating their return, they were far from efficient and alert.

She was handcuffed, but she could still move her hands. The soldier seated on her left was asleep, his wallet sticking out of his pocket. Ever so slowly, she wriggled around until she could grab it and took out a wad of American money. Then she couldn't get the wallet back in his pocket, but he awoke and shifted around just enough for her to shove it in. He lit a cigarette, took two puffs on it and then drifted back to sleep. Smoking was not permitted on the plane but the soldiers were indifferent about regulations. Besides, they would enjoy having a stewardess lean over to tell them to put it out. Darlene's eyes were riveted on the burning cigarette. She eased it out of his fingers and hid it in her hand. Then, she nudged the soldier on her right.

"I have to use the washroom. Excuse me…I have to…"

He awoke and cursed her. Then let his hands wander over her as he undid the handcuffs. Lust was written all over his face as she walked to the washroom.

There, Darlene threw the cigarette in the waste towel bin, which was full of damp paper towels. She shoved in a wad of toilet paper, then returned to her seat. Both soldiers were asleep, so she just sat between them and waited.

It took a while, perhaps ten minutes before someone screamed that they could smell smoke. A stewardess hurried past Darlene one way and then rushed back to the washroom. When she opened the door, smoke billowed out. Huge clouds of it soon filled the entire cabin. The stewardess notified the captain, who announced that he was preparing for an emergency landing. They were right over Düsseldorf, in Germany.

The soldiers awoke and one on the right began putting the cuffs back on Darlene. A stewardess told him that the prisoner had to have her hands free in case she needed to slide down the emergency chute. He snarled foully at her but left the manacles off.

When the plane landed in the middle of a field, the soldiers were advised that they and their prisoner should disembark first. When the door was opened and the chute in place, one soldier went down. Darlene was supposed to go next so as to be between them.

She slid down, tumbling head over heels and slammed into the soldier standing tight against the foot of the chute knocking him down. She shot upright, kicked him in the head and tried to get his gun. Not finding it, she grabbed his wallet and fled into the night.

There were fire trucks, police cars, and ambulances everywhere. Thankfully, she was wearing a black jacket and jeans, which made her almost inconspicuous as she fled. Surrounded by darkness, she circled the downed plane and headed for the terminal, determined to escape. After a few wrong turns, she found an idling shuttle bus, so she scrambled on, paid the driver using money in the stolen wallet, and took a seat. If he left immediately, she would surely escape, but he didn't. He sat reading a newspaper, waiting. A stream of people boarded and took seats around Darlene, whose heart was in her mouth.

Finally, when she was about ready to scream with frustration, he closed the doors and slowly moved away. She hunched over, hoping no one would notice her. Every time the bus stopped, fear bubbled up. Finally, all the other passengers were gone, and the driver announced that he had reached his destination. She had checked the wallet and found it full of American money. Along with what she had taken from the other soldier, she had several hundred dollars, but she had no documents. Nor did she know what city or country she was in. But she knew exactly what she wanted and where to find it.

The driver had parked beside a huge monolith of a hotel. Should she enter and make enquiries? She decided not and instead began walking. It was now 1 a.m. by her watch. After three blocks, she came to a pub with rooms above. She entered and ordered a beer in English, then asked the bartender, "What time is it?"

"In Düsseldorf the time is exactly 4 a.m." He grinned at her. You have vacant rooms?"

"Yeah. You want one?"

"I have to get some sleep. I had a fight with my husband."

"Its twenty-five dollars American, or do you have Euros?"

"I have American." She extended some money. He took this, pulled out a ledger for her to sign, and that was it. Taking her drink, she headed upstairs to figure out what to do next. She couldn't sleep.

So, she was in Dusseldorf, in the middle of a nightmare. What ever was she going to do? Long after the day had dawned, she made her way down stairs to discover that there was a dining area. Going in, she inquired about breakfast. The fat woman she addressed looked at her watch pointedly and said, "Fifteen minutes more that's all." Darlene hurried to a counter where she discovered the food cooked and waiting: ham, eggs, and even grapefruit. She loaded a plate and found a table. The woman came over with her hand out. Darlene dug out some money and looked up inquiringly.

"Ten euros." She handed over a ten-dollar note. The woman huffed off and returned with change. Two young men came in just then and the woman almost screamed at them, "No-no-no! Too late." She tried to block them, but they came to the table where Darlene was and threw themselves into chairs.

"How'd you get served?"

"She gave me fifteen minutes to eat. Go help yourselves, she won't mind. I'll tell her you're with me." They went to the counter. The woman was swearing and muttering in German. She stared at them with hostility. When they were seated she again came to collect.

When they had paid and were shoving food down, the blond one said, "My name's Carl, with a "C". Where're you from?"

"How do you know I'm from anyplace?"

"Well, anyone can see you're American. So are we."

"Do you have a car?"

"Ye-e-s, where do you want to go?"

"France. I'll pay you."

"We wouldn't take your money, there's other ways of paying us." They knew that she knew what they were talking about. *So it's that way, huh?* she thought to herself.

"When do you want to go?"

"The sooner the better."

"Fine. Jeff and I will go pack some bags, and we'll meet you here in…let's say an hour. Is that OK?"

"Sure, I'll be right here unless the woman kicks me out. In that case, I'll be in the bar." Carl and Jeff left. Darlene sat munching the rest of her breakfast, avoiding the woman's glaring stare. She couldn't stay there, Darlene was told a few minutes later, the room was closing. Shrugging, she gathered herself and moved to the bar. She ordered a beer and suddenly began thinking about her daughters and, of course, Mike. Despite herself, she began sobbing.

"Are you all right?" The fat bartender sat her beer in front of her. "Hey what's the problem here?" Darlene finally realized he was speaking to her. His English could use improvement. She rubbed her eyes and looked up.

"I — -I — -I'm fine. I just have moments." She grabbed the beer and downed half of it. He watched her narrowly before going to another customer.

When the two young Americans returned, they were holding a newspaper and laughing. When they were seated, one on each side of Darlene, Carl thrust the newspaper at her.

"The price has gone up my dear." Darlene was staring at the front page where a bad likeness of her stared back. Carl seemed to be the one in charge, and it was he who promised that they could get her across borders even though she had no documents.

"When we get to France, my love, I can introduce you to a guy who will help you with papers. The only thing is, baby, you're going to have to pay. Let's finish up here and get started. I can't wait to start collecting our reward." Jeff laughed uproariously at the thought of the trip.

"We'll take care of you and then baby, you'll be nice." Outside was a Honda, brown and beat up. It would be cramped, but she didn't think they would mind that. She had nothing to carry with her and took the back seat so that she could rest. The Americans knew their way around with Carl driving, and in no time they reached the autobahn. A short time later, they approached a border, and Carl told Darlene to get down on the floor. The guards viewed the little car with barely a glance, and then they were hurtling along again. Jeff sat in the passenger seat but spent most of his time looking over his shoulder at Darlene and grinning.

Through Belgium, and then another border. For some reason, the soldiers, when confronted by the two young Americans, just waved them through with Darlene hunkered down out of sight. It was a long and torturous trip for her. By the time they reached the outskirts of Paris, it was nearly dawn. Jeff and Carl took turns driving and sleeping in the front. Darlene slept fitfully in the back.

Jeff drove straight to a modest but upscale hotel. He registered for them, and Darlene dragged herself behind them as they climbed to the third floor room. They ordered breakfast from room service. Darlene was famished but could hardly eat. Her mind was filled with the upcoming horror: this was pay-time and she searched her mind for a way to escape what lay ahead. They ordered brandy, lots of it, and it was only with the brandy that she was able to even think of letting them at her. The three of them were in the room most of the day. First Jeff went at her, and when he was through, Carl eagerly took over.

It was almost dark when they emerged from the hotel, their needs satisfied. They drove Darlene to an industrial area where trucks were loading up to make the trip to Britain. On foot, they searched for and found a thin, dark young man who greeted the Americans warmly. In exchange for just about all of her money, he would provide her with fake documents so that she could enter not only Britain but Canada as well. He would also provide passage on one of the transports. Her new name was Marlene Gooding. She'd have to remember that.

The passport indicated that she was born in "Moose Jaw Saskatchewan". It took some fast talking to convince her that this wasn't just a mean joke. Without incident, Darlene ended up in a truck yard in London. There were five other people hidden in the truck full of cardboard boxes. When the truck stopped and the door was opened, she burst out. Without a word, she fled the yard into the city, not having a clue where on earth she was or would go.

It was late afternoon. The sky was leaden and felt like rain. Darlene, now almost broke, walked dejectedly along an empty street. What she needed more than anything was a stiff drink. She walked three blocks before she came to a pub. It wasn't just any pub, though. There were by her count, twenty-seven motorcycles parked in front of and alongside the run-down, faded building. It simply said, "The Lamb and Flag" over the door. She walked into a gloomy but noisy interior. It had all the fixtures of an English pub. A couple of tables with two chairs each. Men stood shoulder to shoulder forcing her to squeeze between two hairy giants to attract the bartender's attention.

"Beer." was all she muttered when he got to her.

"Luv…we serve over twenty-five different beers in this pub. Could you be a little more specific?" It was then that Darlene realized the bartender was female. Nothing else had warned her. She eventually managed to be specific enough and the woman pulled her a beer.

The place was full of men. Heavy-knit sweaters, mean faces and dark trousers pretty much described every one of them. She couldn't spot any other women at all. There was a curtained doorway at the far end of the room. A man came out of it looking absolutely evil. He wore a long beige coat, a white shirt and a dark tie. A neatly trimmed goatee completed his appearance. Darlene's eyes followed him as he made his way across the room. She took a swallow of beer and waited. He took his time, stopping occasionally to whisper a few words to someone. When he got to where Darlene was, he forced his way in alongside her.

"You are American right? Are you in trouble? You look like you're in some kind of trouble." Darlene stared at him coldly. Did she look as if she was in trouble? She didn't think so.

"If I was in some kind of trouble, could you help me?" Her voice was filled with defiance.

"I don't know. What kind of trouble? I help people sometimes.

They reimburse me well. Tell me what troubles you."

"I have to get to Canada, and I'm almost broke."

"I see. If I provided you with a plane ticket, would that help?"

"Why would you do that? I told you, I'm almost broke."

"There's other ways to pay. You are very attractive. The cost of a plane ticket is nothing." Rage reared up in Darlene. She knew exactly what the man wanted and she wasn't going to do that again. However…she desperately wanted a plane ticket. She wasn't going to use her body to get it, though. But he didn't know that.

"I need a refill." The man immediately ordered a round. A beer for her and a scotch for himself. They talked in low voices until the deal was set. The man, who now called himself Leon, left to make arrangements. Darlene watched the barmaid serving customers as she tried to figure out how she was going to manage. The barmaid came by her.

"I'd like another and something else."

"What?"

"I notice you have a pin in your hair. Would you sell it to me?"

"What do you want wi' it?"

"I just have to have one and yours is the only one I know of. Please…" The woman extracted it from a windup of brown hair that cascaded down past her shoulders.

"Two quid…that's what I want."

"I only have American."

"OK five dollars. That's about the equivalent. It's one of my better ones. That's why it's two quid."

"Here. And take what I owe for the beer too." Darlene handed over one of her few remaining bank notes. She slipped the pin into her hair after rolling it up just as the barmaid had done.

Sometime later, Leon returned. The bar wasn't any less crowded, and he had had to force his way beside her again. He displayed a ticket, not to Toronto or Montreal, but to Vancouver. Darlene was mystified.

"Why Vancouver?"

"It's the one that's available first thing in the morning. You have to be at the airport at 5 a.m."

"Heathrow?"

"Yes and here's how to get there." He proceeded to lay out all the details for her. Darlene counted on her memory to absorb what he said.

"Can we get something to eat first?"

"Sure, I suppose so. Have you decided on something?"

"I'd like curried chicken English style if that's all right." He ordered from the barmaid for both of them, then ran his hand down her backside. She cringed but not noticeably so. When they finished, he took her by the hand and led her out of the pub. It was fully dark. She held his hand, following him along the narrow sidewalk for three blocks His rooms were on the second floor of a brick house. It appeared dark and empty as he slid the key into the lock. As he led her up the dimly lit stairs, she whispered, "Does anyone else live here?"

"Yes, but they are probably out." he replied in a gruff voice. She almost jumped when he spoke in his full voice because the house seemed so quiet and gloomy. In the apartment, Leon immediately began ridding himself of his overcoat, tie and shirt. He looked quizzically at Darlene as if to say, *C'mon, get started.*

"Do you have anything to drink? I work better with a shot or two." He reached behind him and produced a bottle of schnapps.

"It's all I've got, drink up and let's get physical." By now, he was down to his shorts. His body was thin and white, decidedly ugly to her; even worse, his chest was covered with black hair. When he was completely naked, he eased himself down on the sofa and smirked.

"C'mon it's your turn. Let's get on with it." She undressed slowly. While wild thoughts raced through her head, she did a small bump-and-grind for him. He grinned from ear to ear and slobber ran down his mouth. He indicated for her to kneel beside the sofa. She started to and then leaned over as if to kiss him. The hair-pin was concealed in her hand. Her lips were almost touching his when with full force, she rammed the pin into his left eye. He screamed a blood- curdling scream that might have been heard for blocks. Darlene grabbed a cushion and put it over his face. She held it while he bounced about in vain. Finally, without further noise, he lay still.

She straightened up, picked up her clothes and without taking her eyes off him, got dressed. When she was again decent, she searched his pants and found his wallet as well as the plane ticket. In the wallet was a wad of English pound notes. She grinned to herself. After wiping everything down so that she'd left no prints, Darlene returned to the pub, got a room, and retired for the night. She also gave the hairpin back to its rightful owner.

20

Mike Strong listened, a deep frown on his face. His supervisor was on the phone, having called him at 2 a.m. "She's disappeared, Mike. They don't have a clue as to her whereabouts. She set a fire in the plane over Germany and when it landed, she took off. I just got the bulletin."

"My poor, poor wife…alone in Germany without any money, passport or clothing. What's going to happen to her, Charles? What should I or can I do?"

"You can do nothing. It's just a heads up in case she contacts you. She's still wanted Mike, not only by them but by us over here, too. If she contacts you, Mike, you have to remember, you're a police officer. I'll let you know if we hear any more about this."

When Darlene arrived in Toronto, it was snowing. She had to transfer to another plane that would take her to Vancouver. With her documents, she had no trouble going through Customs. She found out that her next flight was in three hours, so she headed for the correct gate where she sank into a seat to wait.

In Vancouver, she simply found her way out of the airport to a shuttle bus that would take her into the city. She had changed all her money into Canadian currency and was in her mind "set".

The shuttle bus made several stops and then came to the Hotel Vancouver. The driver informed her that she had to get off there as he had reached his destination. She was without luggage and completely at sea.

"Is there like a tourist information center around here?"

"Yeah. You go down Burrard Street half a block. They'll help you." Darlene stepped out of the little bus. It was very breezy, raining and bitterly cold. She cursed under her breath and went to the corner so she could see which street was Burrard. Sorted out, she walked slowly down the hill until there it was right in front of her, the Vancouver Tourist and Information Centre. Excited that she had accomplished something, she entered and approached one of the young female attendants.

"Hi. I just got into town. Could you tell me how to get to the "Y"? I also want to find out where an employment agency is if there is such a thing." The girl smiled at her.

"As it happens, the "Y" is just down Burrard about two blocks. The employment centre is on Howe, which is the next street over. It runs the same way as Burrard. Here I'll give you the address. I'd also like your name and where you are from, so I can write it down. We record each visit."

"Do you have a map?"

"We don't sell maps here but I do have a little one of the downtown area. You can get a larger map from a convenience store."

"Thank you. My name is Marlene Gooding and I just got here from Toronto. She watched the girl dutifully record that, then she left and continued down the street to the "Y". After she'd registered for a room, she sank into a seat in the coffee shop and ate. A glance at her watch told her it was just about noon. She wondered if the employment agency closed for lunch.

Passing a small retail outlet, she noticed that there were umbrellas for sale. She had never owned such a device, but the rain was annoyingly persistent, so she went in and selected a dark colored one. Then she continued on, searching for the address written down for her.

She walked right by the place and then asked a pedestrian if she knew where it was. The woman smiled.

"Dearie, it's right behind you. Look up there." Darlene looked. There it truly was, Canada Employment Centre. Thanking the lady, she went in. It looked jumbled but when she got oriented, she discovered that there were several "boards" with jobs listed on them. She stood reading the various positions available until her legs ached. There was, in the end, only one position that stood out.

A general store in a place called "Hixon" was looking for someone to manage the place. She copied down the details and sought out a clerk.

"Oh you're interested in *that*? It's been posted for weeks, but no one wants it."

"Where is this Hixon?"

"Ha! You won't want the job when you find that out. It's not much more than a railroad siding outside of Prince George on the CN line. Still interested?"

"Yes. I just don't even know where Prince George is or how to get there."

"Well, first you have to call this Mrs. Krakowski and talk to her. If she wants you, you have to take a bus to Prince George and then go by train to Hixon. There's a special phone you can use to call her right over there."

"Thanks I'll be right back." Darlene went to the phone and dialed as per instructions.

"Hello…Hixon store."

"Hello. My name is Marlene. Do you have a vacancy for a store manager?"

"Yes…yes I do. Where are you calling from?"

"I'm in Vancouver. I'm calling from the employment agency." After a lengthy and exhaustive interview over the phone, Darlene was told that she could come to Hixon if she wished. Her expenses would be reimbursed when she got there even if she didn't take the position. It seemed so far to be exactly what she was looking for.

When she arrived back at the Y, she asked the clerk for directions to a public library. Then she made her way there to see if she couldn't find out where Hixon was or at least, where Prince George was located. Darlene couldn't get anywhere without asking directions and the library was no different. She finally arrived on an upper floor where a librarian pulled out a detailed map of the province and even showed her exactly where Prince George was located. Hixon was a different problem but between the two of them, they finally found it. She returned to her room exhausted but excited about her future. But as she lay on her bed, her thoughts drifted to her children, her mother, and lastly Mike. Soon, she was sobbing into the pillow, unable to push away the terrible depression that overcame her. Eventually, she slept.

She awoke at about 4 a.m. It was pouring rain, dark and depressing. Darlene lay in her bed listening to the rain and wishing that she was once again with her children. Eventually, she got up and took a long, hot shower. As she toweled herself dry, she planned her day, then wandered down to the main floor at about 6 a.m. and discovered that she could have breakfast. She did so and then asked directions to the bus depot.

Collecting her precious umbrella, she set out. It was a long hike to another part of town, and she was coming to the conclusion she was lost when she spotted the depot. She went in and approached the ticket window.

"Good morning Miss...wet out there isn't it?"

"Yes and cold. I'd like a ticket to Prince George, please. When does the bus leave?"

"Prince George, huh? Would that be one way?"

"Yes."

"The bus leaves in an hour from bay four. Have a nice trip." Darlene glanced at her watch and then went to locate bay four. When she was satisfied, she headed for the coffee shop to have a last cup of coffee before she boarded. It was a ten-hour trip.

It snowed from a town called Hope onward, and when she arrived at her destination, it was dark as well. Right next to the bus depot was a bar. Darlene headed in and ordered a scotch, which she downed in two gulps. Then she asked directions to the train station. There were quite a few people on the sidewalks, heads down to avoid the snow as they walked. When she found the station, she went in and stepped up to a window.

"Hi…is anybody here?" She waited, apparently the only person in the building. Then a short, fat guy waddled out of a back room..

"Ye-e-s can I help you?"

"Can I catch a train from here to Hixon?"

"Hixon? You sure you want to go there? There's not much there."

"A woman has a store there. She wants someone to run it and I'm applying for the job."

"Well, there's a train we call "the local". It leaves here tomorrow at 5 a.m. and goes to McBride. Hixon's on the way. Do you want a one way or return?"

"One way, thank you." When Darlene had her ticket, she went across the street to get a room. The place had a bar so, when she finished with the room booking, she went down to the bar for supper and some refreshment.

The next morning, Darlene woke with a splitting headache. She cursed quietly and popped a couple of Tylenol that she had been carrying around ever since the last drug store she'd managed to find. She had a quick shower and with a paper cup of coffee from a kiosk, she rushed over to catch her train. The trip was uneventful and when she got off the train carrying only an umbrella, Inga was standing there waiting for her.

Well, not her exactly. Inga met every train that came through. As soon as she spotted Darlene, she smiled broadly.

"Are you Marlene?"

"Yes. Are you Mrs. Krakowski?"

"Nobody calls me that. I'm Inga. Come over to the store. Have you had lunch?"

"I didn't even have breakfast actually. The train left at 5 a.m. All I had was a coffee."

"Well, it's lunch time anyway so I'll throw something together and we can talk." Darlene paused to look around. It was spectacular. There was a mountain seemingly right in front of her, then a few colorful little houses in the distance, and the store. That was all. Between the railway and the store was a road, probably the one by which a person could drive to Prince George.

The store dominated the immediate area. It was a one-storey building that had been added on to a few times and it looked huge. There was an area on one side with a hitch rack for horses and another area where people could camp. Inga didn't have to unlock it, she just walked in and a little bell rang when the door opened.

Inside, it was a jumble of products for sale. There was far too much for the eye to take in, but Darlene spotted metal tubs and pails hanging from the ceiling. There were numerous shelves of canned food. In the back was a living area with an extra bedroom. Inga led Darlene there and invited her to sit at a kitchen table while she prepared lunch.

"Well Marlene, what's your immediate reaction to Hixon? Do you think you could live here?"

"Yes. It's exactly what I'm looking for."

"You're not running away from the law are you?" They'll find you here, too, if you are."

"I'm running away from a bad marriage that's all. I was looking for someplace quiet where I could heal."

"It must have been bad."

"Bad enough." Darlene looked out the window at the mountain wistfully. While they ate, Inga described the work that she would do on a daily basis.

"There's a spare room here. I want you to just hang around a couple of days to see what you think of the place. If you like it and decide to stay for a long time, I'll pack up and split. You'll be on your own then."

"The first thing I'd like to do is crash for an hour or so. I didn't get much sleep last night and woke up with a headache. I'm just about wiped out."

"Sure. Have a nap. Then I'll show you the books and stuff. You'll have to send me an accounting every month, and you'll have to order supplies and pay for them. It's a lot of work, but you've got all of every day to do it."

"OK I'll join you in a bit." Darlene went into the bedroom, closed the door and sank onto the bed. She wished she could sleep, but thoughts of her children haunted her. Two hours later, after a shallow nap, she came out to find Inga sitting on a stool doing paper work.

"Hi. You're not a drinker are you…or a druggie or anything? I need somebody reliable." Darlene looked out the window at the snow.

"No. I'm not any of those things. I'm ready to take over here if you want. Just show me where everything is, show me the books and then, I'll be the person you're looking for. This is where I want to be." A broad smile appeared on Inga's face.

"I have been looking for so long for somebody that would say that..." She slid off the stool and went to the back. Darlene was left alone in the store. She wandered among the shelves as she contemplated her future. An hour passed. There was no sign of Inga. It was deathly quiet. Darlene decided that not a single vehicle had used the road since she got off the train. She was sure of it because she would have heard any motor. Inga came out.

"I'm just about packed. I wrote down where you are, to send my share of the profits if there are any each month."

"How often do you get a customer?

"There's a few each day. Somebody's sure to come in around suppertime. If anybody wants a coffee, you make it and charge for it." Then she began teaching Darlene all about running the store. Sure enough, a native lady entered the store just before dark. She picked out a few items and welcomed Darlene to Hixon.

"I hope you like it here, we need new blood." Smiling, she left.

"Was that the supper rush?"

"You'll get used to it. Find a hobby to do when it's quiet."

"Like what?

"Try writing, knitting or painting. If you're any good, you could have a second career." She grinned. "Tomorrow the train goes back through here. I'm going with it." That night, Darlene didn't go to bed until midnight. Her head was full of information and she was looking forward to taking over. She slept fitfully. At 5a.m. Inga was up, making coffee and finishing her packing. She had outlined all the procedures that Darlene was expected to follow. Now, she was catching the train and heading for Florida. The fact that it was snowing heavily only added to this determination.

The train came, and Inga received a sendoff from dozens of people who had suddenly discovered that she wasn't going to be there anymore. Darlene stood watching the train until it was out of sight. Then, she went back to the store and settled herself into the suite that Inga had occupied. She made breakfast and wondered what the day would bring.

As usual, she began thinking of Victoria, Joanie and Mike. She stared at the phone sitting on the table. Beckoning her, daring her, taunting her. It would be so easy. She knew the number by heart, knew *all* the numbers no matter where Mike might be. Choking back sobs, she sat and cursed the fate that had brought her to where she was.

Darlene spent much time of her familiarizing herself with the items she had for sale. The store seemed to have every imaginable thing someone might want. No matter what might be required, it was likely there somewhere. People who came in for things would sometimes stare at her brazenly, waiting for her to make a mistake, but she didn't.

"I know you got it here somewhere, an' I need it real bad." This became almost the by-word of everyone who came to the store.

Together, they and Darlene would begin searching until the item was found. Often it was right in front of them and they'd have a laugh over it. Darlene never had to hunt down the same item twice.

One of the first orders she issued for supplies included an order for suitable clothing for herself. She could get what she needed now, and she needed practically everything.

Darlene had made no reference to her background, and no one in the community had any idea she was a nurse. She intended to keep it that way. However, she couldn't resist explaining what various over-the-counter drugs were for and in many cases, which one was best. Slowly, she got a reputation for being, "one smart woman".

One afternoon, an RCMP officer entered the store. Darlene's heart was in her mouth. He poured himself a coffee and introduced himself as Ted Ryan. Darlene said she was "Marlene" and stopped right there. Ted was in uniform, friendly and courteous.

"I'm going to stay here in your extra bedroom overnight like I always do, and tomorrow I'll drift around to see if anyone has a problem. I'll head for Penny around lunchtime. Krakow didn't tell you about me?"

"No. Is her name Krakow? I thought she was Inga."

"Her last name is Krakowski and every body calls her Krakow. The department has an arrangement with her to put an officer up when he visits town. It's probably in with your other paperwork if you want to check."

"Oh no, I'll take your word for it. If I ever talk to her again, I'll ask her but she told me, 'Don't call me, I'll call you.'"

"That's her, she wanted out of here real bad."

"Why was she here if she hated it so much?"

"She didn't tell you? Her uncle owned this store. He passed away and left it to her. She's a university grad and wants to live in Florida. That's where she was living when this store got dumped in her lap. She's a toxicologist with the university down there."

"No, she didn't tell me any of that stuff."

"Are you married? I hope you don't mind my asking."

"No, that's all right. The truth is, I'm divorced. I had a bad marriage and came here to find a quiet place where I can get over it."

"Well, it's sure quiet. If that's what you want you've got it.

Where're you from?"

"Is that the police officer asking or are you just inquisitive?" He just smiled. "I'm not from anywhere. I've just been around a few times." After he finished his coffee, he left but said he'd return in time for supper. Darlene sniffed to herself and wondered how this new factor would affect her life.

Going through the filing cabinet to check on Constable Ryan, Darlene discovered that she was also in the firearms business. She giggled when she found suppliers listed who sold handguns. She also found the contract with the RCMP, which outlined the agreement Ted had referred to.

Having little else to do, she flipped through a catalogue from an arms supplier. Fascinated with the variety, she filled out the order form in the catalogue and ordered a 9 mm police issue automatic. It was supposed to be ordered to be sold through the store but in reality, it was going to be exclusively hers even though she didn't have an owner's permit. She had no intention of applying for one either.

The evening went well. Ted came for supper, complimented her on the meal and disappeared. "I'll be back about midnight" were his parting words. Darlene went to bed, leaving the door to the store unlocked and a nightlight on. She was awakened in the morning, by the smell of freshly brewed coffee. After taking a shower and dressing, she entered the kitchen to find the constable preparing pancakes.

"It's a wonder you're not married with your talents." She grinned.

"I just never found anyone who suited my tastes" he replied as he handed her a plate with a short stack on it.

"When I was in university, I worked as a short order cook to pay my way. I've made thousands of pancakes in my time."

"How'd you become a police officer?"

"It's what I always had in mind, but I studied criminology first to give myself an edge. It has helped some but out here in the boonies, I really don't get to use what I've learned."

"You're not planning to stay in this district?"

"Nope. I want to get to a big city where I can do some good. I'm just a baby-sitter here. Nothing ever happens out here in the bush."

"Hm-m you never can tell though, can you?" *I better shut up!* she thought.

Constable Ryan made a few more visits, came for lunch, and then left, thanking Darlene for her hospitality.

He was driving a massive 4-wheel drive vehicle especially marked to identify his official status.

A week later, a pile of supplies was off-loaded from the train. A young native boy of about eighteen brought it all to the store. When Darlene unpacked everything, she found her gun along with the ammunition she had ordered. She cleaned and loaded the weapon before hiding it under the counter where the cash register was. Weeks went by, spring came, and the snow started to disappear.

One of her frequent customers was a big, rawboned man named Gunther. He had a ranch somewhere near the river that ran along the base of the mountains visible from the store. He was cold when he first met Darlene, but gradually came to accept her as the store manager. When she couldn't immediately find what he wanted, he'd remark about how much he missed Krakow.

One morning he came in after carefully cleaning the mud off his shoes. He had a list that he handed Darlene. Then he poured a coffee while she began filling the order.

"My wife insists that I bring you out to the ranch for a steak supper. When could you come?"

"That's wonderful. I could come today. What's her name?"

"Dottie. We used to have Krakow out about once a month. You could stay overnight because the road is dangerous in the dark."

"Dangerous?"

"Yeah. There's a couple of places where it's narrow with a steep drop-off. It wouldn't matter if you locked up an' came with me; that's what Krakow did."

"I'll just grab a few things. So I'm going to stay over night?"

"Yep. If you feel comfortable with that." Darlene disappeared to pack. Then she took her duffle to the front of the store and slipped her gun into it. She would transfer it to her purse later. She checked everything, locked up and climbed into Gunther's red Ford F150. It was roomy inside and she could tell it was a serious machine when he started it. They did a turn around the store, picked up a narrow little track and headed towards the mountains.

It was a scenic three quarters of an hour drive mainly because the road was so bad that he couldn't get any speed up. When they arrived, Darlene was shocked to see so many buildings nestled in the hills. She could also see the Fraser River in the background. A handsome young woman came out to greet them.

"That's Dottie. Then there's Patricia but I call her "Wiggles" She hates it but laughs about it. She's ten."

"Hi". Dottie said warmly. "Come, I'll show you where to put that bag. I'm so glad you could join us. You must get lonely stuck in that store by yourself." Darlene obediently followed her down a hallway to the guest bedroom, or at least one of them — the place was huge.

"We're having lunch in about twenty minutes. I have some moose meat that I'm making into sandwiches if you're interested." Dottie turned and left Darlene alone in the room. As soon as the door was closed, she transferred the gun into her large purse. *I hope nothing makes me use this, but I'm damned well going to be ready.* After freshening herself up she made her way to the kitchen.

"Just have a seat there. You know that in the country, most socializing is done in the kitchen. Oh, here's Patricia. Patricia…come say hi to Marlene." The girl entered the room with a bounce.

"Hi. You're the store lady."

"Uh-huh I took over from Krakow. Did you know Krakow?"

"Sure. She used to come here all the time. She used to bring a rifle and shoot with Dad. Do you shoot?"

"Some."

"Sure she does. She picked up a gun when she was packing. It's probably in her purse right now."

Patricia's eyes were as big as saucers. "You weren't supposed to see that."

"Expecting trouble? I bet you don't have a permit for it. Can you use it?"

"I'm just paranoid. I've seen my share of trouble. I don't have a permit for it but I can use it. I shouldn't have brought it I guess."

"Well, it pays to be careful. After we eat, I want to set up a couple of targets. I want to see if you can hit anything." Darlene didn't respond. She knew she was in a pickle. If she showed her expertise, they would certainly wonder about her background. Now, she really wished she hadn't brought it.

The lunch passed smoothly. A young man named "Blaze" joined them and he spent most of the lunch eyeballing Darlene. When Dottie asked her how she liked the moose, she replied, "I like it 'cause it isn't gamy. Some wild meet is too gamy for me." It must have been the right answer because Gunther chuckled appreciatively.

During the meal, Darlene could barely keep her eyes off the little girl, Patricia. *She looks so much like Vicki I can hardly stand it,* Darlene thought bitterly. She couldn't keep her eyes from filling with tears and hoped that no one would notice.

After lunch, Gunther brought out two bulls eye targets made of paper. He pinned them up on pieces of plywood set in place for that purpose.

"Now, little lady, let's see what you can do with that firearm you're packing." Darlene still didn't know how she was going to handle it. She could *try* to shoot badly and have them laugh at her. Finally, she decided that she would just be herself. Simpler that way. Gunther pointed out a line that was 50 feet from the targets. Darlene stood quietly.

She brought her gun up and shot four times, so fast it sounded like one long shot. In the target, smack in the center there appeared four little holes. They were placed so that all four could be covered with a silver dollar. Gunther stared at her work, then started taking the targets down.

"Aren't you going to shoot?"

"Lady on my best day I couldn't come close to what you just did. You must have some background to be able to shoot like that. Blaze stood watching, a smirk on his face. Gunther didn't invite him to participate.

"Could you autograph this target for me? I ain't seen nothing like that in my whole life. I'm going to keep it so I can brag I seen it. Let's get the horses, see if you can ride." He took the signed target, carefully folded it and carried it back to the shed he got it from. Darlene had scrawled, "Marlene Gooding", hoping that whoever read it wouldn't be able to make it out.

They went down to the stable, where several horses were penned.

Gunther put ropes on three and tied them to the rails of the corral. "Can you saddle up?" he asked Darlene.

"Sure…I guess so."

"Well, here then. He showed her which saddle to use.

"Put it on the black, that's yours for the afternoon." She threw the saddle over her shoulder and went to obey. He watched as she worked and when she gave the horse a gentle knee in the side to rid it of excess air, he nodded approvingly. She mounted and swung the horse around. Blaze and Gunther led off as they made their way towards the river. It seemed to be about a half-mile ride. The ride reminded her of her previous station in life and again, her eyes filled with tears.

"This's the Fraser." Gunther mouthed when they arrived at water's edge. It was flat at that point so that there seemed to be a small beach. The trail led along the river and as they rode, Darlene gazed at the wide stretch of turbulent water. She watched eddies form, and shuddered at how dangerous a river it appeared to be.

That night at supper, Patricia excitedly asked Darlene,

"Did you ride Monty? That's my horse. He's the black one. I ride with Dad sometimes."

"Yes. I rode the black one. Did he ever buck you off?"

The girl grinned. "No. He's a gentle giant. That's what I call him."

After supper, Darlene offered to help with the dishes. She cleaned the table off then did the drying while Patricia trotted beside her explaining where everything went. When all was done, Gunther brought out a deck of cards. They spent the evening playing hearts and sipping drinks. Patricia and Blaze were confined to sodas while the adults had whatever they wanted from the well-stocked bar. Darlene sipped a glass of scotch for most of the evening. She was the first one to glance at her watch and say she wanted to hit the sack.

The next morning, after a large country-style breakfast, Gunther informed Darlene that Blaze would drive her back to Hixon. Her heart quickened uneasily, as he had continued ogling her throughout the previous evening. Would having him drive her back be a wise decision? She put her bag in the vehicle and climbed into the cab. Blaze, already in, fired up and they were off.

She had to give him credit, he tried to be amiable, but he was nervous. They arrived at a fork in the road and Blaze turned left.

"Is this the road to the store? I don't remember a turn like that."

"I thought I'd show you the lake that lies almost completely on the ranch."

"Turn around. I don't want to see any lake. I have to get back."

"It'll only take a minute." Darlene reached into her bag for her gun. She held it in his face.

"Turn this bloody thing around! I don't want to see the damned lake. I saw the way you were eyein' me so turn around now!"

"Don't you point that thing at me!" But he stopped the truck and began a U-turn.

"You think you're some hot stuff. I don't need you." Darlene didn't waver. She had her finger on the trigger with the gun pointed at his head. Her hand was almost in her lap but she couldn't miss. He finally got turned around and floored it. The truck bounced wildly until he slowed.

"Stupid bitch…you think I'd be after a scrawny thing like you?"

"Just shut up and drive. I'll do my explainin' to Gunther." Now that they were again on the right road, she began to relax. She said not a word until he pulled up at the store. Then, she got out, secured her bag and slammed the door of the vehicle. As he sped off, she put the gun back in her bag and entered the store.

It seemed cold in the store, cold, quiet, and lonely after her visit to the ranch despite Blazes's stupid antics. Putting her bag away, she poured herself a stiff drink and thought about how close she had come to losing everything. She stared at the phone, the phone that taunted her constantly. *What if I just called Mike now? If he was at home I could maybe talk to Vicki or Joanie. Oh GOD let me talk to them.* Her hand reached out. Should she chance it? Drawing her hand back, she took a swallow of scotch and thought.

After a few moments, she sank onto the chair by her desk. It was quiet. No one was around. Her mind drifted back to Newark. She could visualize everything just as she had last seen it. Slowly, she picked up the phone and with shaking fingers dialed her former home.

21

Mike arrived home from work at 11 p.m. He was tired, short-tempered and looking forward to bed. He unlocked the door, then locked it again once he was inside. Turningon some lights, he armed the alarm panel and wearily shrugged off his jacket. The kids were in bed, being watched over by Dolly, who was camped on the sofa with the TV on but no volume. She was dozing. Mike looked at her with pity. It was tough without Darlene. Just as he poured himself a scotch, the phone rang and his heart sank. So often it was work demanding his presence. He grabbed it on the first ring so as not to wake anyone.

"Yeah?"

"Mike! Is that you?" He stared at the phone. Was he dreaming?

He couldn't tell.

"Baby, is this really you? Where are you? How're you doing? I miss you so much!"

"Mike…oh… Mike… I'm so glad to hear your voice. How's Vicki and Joanie? Are they in bed? I'm fine but I just wanted to let you know that I'm all right." She knew she was babbling but didn't care.

"Where *are* you? They ask every day at the station whether I've heard from you. They want you real bad. I'm not going to turn on you. I'll never tell them you called me, baby, believe it."

"I'm in Canada at a place called Hixon. I have a job taking care of a store. Nobody's looking for me up here."

"I just got in. Dolly's takin' care of the kids, but we all miss you.

I am going to take a few days off. How do I get there?"

"You can't come *here*!"

"Why not? I have to. Baby, I just had the worst shit of a day. Don't say I can't come to see you. *God* I want to hold you so bad. Why can't I come there?"

"I don't know. I…I'd sure love to see you. You'd have to come to Vancouver. Then you'd have to come to Prince George. Are you writing this down?"

"Dolly's got paper. She's right here. I have to go to Prince George?"

"Yeah. Then you have to get on a train. A special train called the local. L-o-c-a-l. It will bring you to Hixon. You know, everybody'd know you're a cop. They'd…they'd…I don't want to have to run again, and I can't go to prison. I can't be locked up, Mike. Please don't let them get me."

"I'll find you. I'll talk to you about things. Maybe we can work something out. I won't tell anyone where you are, but you have to come home. I'll tell you how when I see you. I have to go to bed. This is the best day I ever had. Baby, I love you so much. I miss you. Dolly misses you. The kids miss you so much."

"Mike…I wish I could hold you right now. Don't let them find **me**, Mike. I'll wait for you. I won't sleep tonight. I love you. Bye."

"Bye."

Darlene hung up and sat staring at the phone. Mike was coming to see her. Would he bring the girls? What if he got caught? He'd lose his job! She knew she wouldn't sleep. She poured a healthy slug of scotch, hoping it would relax her. Then she got up and wandered through the store. Everything was so quiet. She could hear her heart beating and put her hand on it. Sipping her drink, she prepared for bed. Through the window, she could see the railway that would bring Mike to her.

The following morning, before she was ready, someone banged on the front door. The door was, of course, locked but apparently somebody needed some item right away. She dressed hurriedly and without even brushing her teeth, went to open the door. It was Gunther.

"Good morning! Did I get you up? I need some stuff." He handed her a list. She took it and began searching for the required items.

"Blaze tells me you got upset wi' him. You pulled your gun."

"He was going to drive me out in the bush. I didn't want to go,
 and he wouldn't listen. I had to get his attention."

"Blaze is a good boy. He wouldn't hurt anyone. I promised his mother I'd take care of him. Maybe you're too handy wi' that thing."

"He was supposed to drive me home. At least that's what I thought. I'm used to being obeyed."

"You aren't going to fit in here wi' an attitude like that. I could tell Constable Ryan to talk to you."

"If you think you have to. I'm not going out in the bush with anybody, especially an over-heated punk."

"That's not fair...he's not like that. Besides, he tells it different."

"Here's your stuff. I'm sorry there wasn't any coffee but I had a hard night. About Blaze — I will try to curb myself. If you have to report me, go ahead." Gunther took the box Darlene had packed and left. His stride was determined and deliberate.

By this time it was fully daylight. Trees were greening, the sun was on the hillside, and Darlene made a point of putting Gunther and Blaze out of her mind. She went at the store's paperwork determined that she would not be intimidated.

22

Scattered over the plain were a half-dozen or more houses in which the railroad workers lived. "Bohunks" some people called them because they came from "the old country" and couldhardly speak English. They were left alone most of the time. The wives shopped at the store but said little. They wore kerchiefs on their heads, winter and summer. A dark-skinned man from this community rushed into the store one morning, not long after Darlene's confrontation with Gunther. He began buying bandages and salves, seeming to just grab whatever was nearest.

"Has someone been hurt?" inquired Darlene in a concerned friendly voice.

"My wife…my wife cut her leg bad. It's bleeding. Can you come?" Darlene flew into action. She packaged what he had bought plus stuff she felt was necessary, then got him to point out his house and hurried to it. Bursting in, she found the short, plump woman sitting with her leg on a chair. It was a bad gash, deep, and Darlene went right to work.

Wordlessly, she cleansed, lubricated and then bound the wound tightly.

"You must go on the train to Prince George. The bandage will hold until you get there." She wasn't sure the woman understood but she nodded as if she did and thanked Darlene. She caught the train when it came through.

The woman's name was Christine Liebo. When she got to the hospital, she was examined by a nurse.

"Who did this? It looks like you've already seen a nurse."

"It's the woman who runs the store. She's not a nurse, just the storekeeper." Christine's English was passable.

"Well, she did a very good job. The doctor will put in some stitches, and then you will be fine. Get the storekeeper to change the bandages in three days. Tell her she should be a nurse, she did well." When Mrs. Liebo got home, she phoned Darlene and told about her visit and what the nurse had said. *I suppose I've put my foot in it. Now people will think I'm a nurse. Ted Ryan might hear about it. I'd sure hate it if I had to run again.*

Then she began thinking about Mike meeting Constable Ryan. *They'd both know the other was a cop, even if Ted didn't wear a uniform. I have to prevent their meeting. I wonder when Mike's getting here.*

The natives that lived around Hixon loved Darlene. They considered her very smart and quizzed her about the medications they bought. Many times she had prevented someone from buying the wrong medication and had described in detail how to treat a malady. In their eyes, she was not just a nurse, but a doctor that came there to treat them.

One morning, shortly before 5 a.m., the telephone brought Darlene awake. It wasn't by her bed but on the desk in the store. A call at that hour she considered important, so in her nightie, she hurried to answer it.

"Hixon General Store."

"Hello, baby, I'm here in Prince George, just about to catch that train you told me to get. I've got Victoria and Joanie with me and we'll be there at about ten."

"Mike!...Mike. Oh I can't wait. Put Vickie on. Hi darling...I can't wait to see you. Are you being a good girl?"

"Yes Mommy. We miss you."

"Is Joanie a good girl?"

"Yes Mommy...where are you?"

"Get on the train. I'm waiting for you, and I'll see you very soon. Put your daddy on. Hi. I guess you better get on that train. I will be here in the store. I usually meet the train, but I don't want to have everybody in town see us meet. Come to the store. Oh I can't wait!" She hung up and stood staring at the phone as she contemplated the problems involved in having her whole family at the store.

When the steam engine propelled train gusted to a stop in front of the store, Darlene was standing at the window watching. First, her two girls emerged and then Mike. He stood looking around for a minute and then began walking to the store. He was wearing a dark sweater and pressed slacks. With his build, Darlene thought that everyone who saw him would automatically think "cop," and this worried her.

They opened the door to enter. Darlene stood out of sight of the people meeting the train. She tried to grin. Her mouth quivered, her arms went out and then she was hugging her girls, tears streaming down her face. She had no words, just tears and then giggles. She stood and flew into Mike's open arms. They held each other tightly while Darlene continued to sob with pure joy, and the girls hugged their parents' legs.

"Come into my place. I've got coffee and pop or whatever you want." She pulled away from Mike and stumbled to the back of the store.

"I might have to serve people. They usually come here from the train. Make yourselves comfortable. Oh God it's so good to see you!"

"How did you find this place? I'm surprised it's on any map. You sure hid yourself: no wonder they can't find you." Mike was laughing as he talked about the efforts of the Russians to track her down.

"Does Frank know where you are? Does anybody?"

"Not a soul. I'd lose my job if anyone ever found out where I am right now. I told everybody I was going to Disneyland. That's where they think we are."

"You're not going to turn me in or try to get me to turn myself in?"

"We are going to talk about that. I've missed you so damned much I don't know how I could have let them take you away, despite what you did."

"We're going to talk about *that* too."

Darlene sat hugging each of her girls so tight they felt squeezed. She and Mike talked and stared at each other in between the times that she had to go out and serve a customer. In the late afternoon, she dug a couple of steaks out of the freezer.

"I got these from Gunther before he got mad at me. It's moose. I hope you like it. I'll have to tell you about Gunther. He has an eighteen year-old kid out there that lusts after me. There's no other word for it. I hope he keeps his distance, but I don't think he will. He tried once and I had to pull on him."

"You have a gun." Mike said it with a finality that indicated he should have known. He sounded defeated.

"I keep it under the cash register. Don't worry, I won't use it, I like it here." Mike pushed Joanie off his lap and walked to the front of the store. He pulled the nickel-plated weapon from its place and examined it.

"Where'd you pick this up?"

"See that rack of rifles there? I have a catalogue and order what ever I'm inclined to. Officially, it belongs in stock but I carry it in my bag."

"You pulled it on this kid?"

"His name's Blaze and I most certainly did. I hope you meet him and put the fear of God in him."

After supper, while Darlene held the kids, she and Mike chewed over many things including the chances of her ever being a housewife again.

"I could get you a really high-powered lawyer and perhaps he might see a way that you could plead self-defense, but it's a long shot. However, I'm not a lawyer.

He might see it entirely different. The question is, are you willing to chance it?"

"Even if I got a few years, I could at least watch my kids grow up. I'm scared Mike. I'm really scared. I don't want to just get dumped into the system and forgotten about. I could never stand that. The first chance I got, I'd run."

After a while, Darlene lay down with her two girls in the extra bedroom until they went to sleep. Then she extracted herself from them and went in to Mike. He was in bed, waiting and ready. She snuggled into his arms, breathed a deep breath and felt so happy, she wasn't sure she could handle it. The door was locked, it was warm in the store, and aside from the noises they made, everything was quiet. Eventually, they slept.

A grinding roar woke Darlene. She thought she was dreaming but it persisted. As she squirmed about, Mike also awoke.

There was some vehicle right outside, racing its engine and grinding gears. Cursing softly, she got up and put a robe on. She peered out. Gunther's big red Ford flashed by, careening around out of sight. Soon it reappeared. Whoever was driving it was doing donuts around the store.

"Mike…" All of a sudden, there was a resounding crash. The whole store shook. Glass tinkled as it fell. The driver had driven right through the front entrance of the store and the truck was parked with three-quarters of it in the store. The driver opened the side door and stumbled out.

"Marlene…I've come to visit you. Where are you?" The voice was high, nervous and shrill. The guy strode on shaky legs towards the living quarters. "Marlene…"

Mike stood watching grimly. He was behind the open door, ready. As Blaze stumbled through the door, Mike grabbed him by the arm.

"OK, asshole, just calm down an' you won't get hurt." Blaze reared up, sending a roundhouse in Mike's direction. Mike drew back and clobbered the youth, possibly cracking his jaw and certainly knocking him cold. He collapsed on the floor, blood running down his chin. Darlene now had some lights on.

"Are we in danger of fire here?"

"I don't think so. Who is this and why'd he call you Marlene?"

"That's Blaze. He's Gunther's hired-hand. I better call Gunther to come get his truck." She made for the phone. Joanie and Vicki stood in their doorway, holding their ears and looking scared. Mike quickly went over and comforted them.

"Hi, Gunther. Your Ford truck is in the middle of my store. Blaze drove it there. How is he? He's out cold. Can you just get in here? OK. Thanks." She went over to her daughters and Mike. "He's on his way. I suppose that seeing as there's no cop around, you're in charge until one gets here. Secure the scene."

And then, "Well, I guess I'm out of business. Now I don't have any place to go, so I suppose I'll try that lawyer of yours. We might as well catch the train in the morning." She sank down on the floor and sobs racked her body. Mike stood, holding Joanie with one arm and cradling Vicki with the other. He looked somberly over the damage and kept an eye on Blaze, who didn't move but was clearly still alive. A half hour later, a vehicle skidded to a stop outside. Blaze was still out. Gunther rushed into the store, stepping over piles of broken glass, easing himself past his truck. He spotted Blaze.

"What happened to him?"

"He wanted to fight."

"Who're you?"

"Superintendent of detectives, New Jersey police."

"You're out of your jurisdiction."

"Until another police officer shows up, I'm the law. I'll thank you to remember that."

"You knocked this boy out?"

"More or less."

"Let's see that badge again. I'm going to bring charges…he's just a kid." Mike held his badge under Gunther's nose. Then, Darlene spoke.

"I'm catching the morning train. Here's Krakow's e-mail, postal address and phone number. I'm through here. I'll pay you if I have to board this place up after you've moved the truck. Then, you can report to Krakow any way you want. You can say I drove the truck in here if you want to. I'm outta here." She pushed a sheet of paper at Gunther, then glanced at Mike.

"I'm going to pack my duds, and then I'll put some coffee on. Supervise the removal of the bloody truck will you?" She turned and on shaking legs, headed for the kitchen. First, she put coffee on. Then, she buried her head in her hands and sobbed. Terrible thoughts ran through her mind, mostly centered on the fact that she was on the move again.

Using a duffle bag that belonged in stock, she packed her clothes. Not bothering to fold anything, she simply threw things in and ran a list through her mind, so that she'd pack everything. Joanie and Vicki came into the bedroom and watched silently, concern on their faces.

"Mommy's going to come live with you again for a little while.

Then I might have to go somewhere else."

"You're coming home?"

"Yes Vicki, for now." She heard the truck start up. Wood cracked, and glass tinkled as Mike eased it backwards out of the store. Gunther had Blaze conscious and sitting up. He worked on the boy, trying to get him on his feet. He spoke softly, cursing and cajoling, as he put an arm around him and lifted him. After settling the boy in the vehicle, he returned.

"You know, I don't understand how come a New Jersey cop just happens to be here in this place at this time. I can't understand that."

"I guess I forgot to explain. Her name isn't Marlene, it's Darlene, and she's my wife and the mother of my kids." Gunther stared at him, his mouth wide open. Finally, he turned away, saying nothing. Darlene heard and she grinned.

After Gunther left, Darlene tried to straighten up the store, but it was a futile gesture. Gunther had acquiesced when she'd asked him to board up the front of the store. It was the only solution she could think of. Months of repairs would be needed before the store could operate again, and she wasn't going to supervise the job. Krakow probably wouldn't want her to anyway. In the meantime, the residents of Hixon were going to have to go elsewhere for their needed supplies.

The train came at a little after noon. This time, Darlene stood proudly with her husband waiting to board. Many of her customers greeted her and got the news about the store. She assured them that Krakow would be contacted, and that all would be done to repair things as soon as possible. She didn't know that, but they needed the assurance. In vivid detail, she described how Blaze had circled the store at 3 a.m. and then driven right through the front entrance. As much as Gunther wanted to downplay the kid's part, she felt that the blame should be laid squarely where it belonged.

They overnighted in Prince George and then again in Vancouver. Mike was familiar with this because he'd had to do it coming the other way. Finally, they caught a Delta Airlines flight to JFK in New York. Darlene was on her way home.

When she finally stepped through the door of her own house, Dolly grabbed her and hugged her tightly.

"I don't know what's going to happen now but I sure am glad you're all right. Hildon is waiting for you in the living room, so you might as well get right to it. I'll bring some coffee."

"Hildon?" She looked at Mike.

"He's a lawyer. I called ahead. You're going to have to surrender yourself real soon, or I'll still lose my job. He's going to familiarize you with the procedure." Darlene sat herself down on her own sofa, the one she had picked out. She could hardly believe she was there.

A silver-haired, distinguished looking man in an expensive suit sat across from her. His eyes twinkled, and there was a bit of a smile of greeting on his mouth. He held some papers and cleared his throat.

"Mrs. Strong…I've began examining the charges against you. The prosecutor almost demands that you surrender in the next half hour. I know you've had a long flight but your surrender is very important. We should go *now*. He stood up, expecting her to follow. She sat looking stunned. Mike grabbed her arm and pulled her to her feet.

"You'll be able to rest once they've processed you, but you better go. Jeff will talk on the way and also after they've finished. Tomorrow there will be a hearing where your bail will be discussed. I'm sorry, honey, but this is the way it works. He held firmly to her arm all the way to Jeff Hildon's silver-blue Jaguar.

"I'll see you in an hour or so. I have to go in and make a report. This has to be done by the book or we both go under. I know you don't want that." He gave her a quick kiss, as Hildon pulled away. Joanie and Vickie watched, fear on their faces. Mike took them inside and began to explain to them as best he could.

It took a full two hours before Darlene was left in an interview room free of everyone but Jeff Hildon. She had been printed, probed and pushed from one process to another, and felt exhausted and terrified. The officers all knew that she was Mike's wife but informed her there would be "no special privileges for her." Now she stared helplessly at her lawyer.

"Do you think I'll get bail?" she whispered. "I think so but it might be expensive."

"I haven't even seen a cell yet. Do you think they'll put me in with other people or in a cell by myself?"

"You'll be alone until after tomorrow. Do you need anything?"

"No. I can manage. What time will you be here in the morning?"

"You'll be brought before a judge at 10 am. I'll see you then."

He stuffed papers into his briefcase, got up and rapped on the door.

It opened and he left. Darlene, in handcuffs again, also went through a door, into an elevator and up to another floor where she was placed in a cell. It contained a wooden bench bolted to the wall and a toilet. There was no shower. As the metal door slammed shut, she sank onto the bench and stared at the floor.

She received a food tray that night and at one in the morning, when she was also allowed to have a shower. Still in the clothes she had come with, she sat and waited, trying not to think.

She had no jewelry, no watch and no idea what time it was. Just as she was ready to scream in frustration, a guard came shuffling down the hallway calling her name. She was handcuffed again and led through walkways to the court. Told to sit with a group of people in a similar situation, she waited again, now finally without handcuffs. Finally, Jeff Hildon entered and took a seat. Then she was told to "rise," and court was in session.

The judge sat where she could hardly see him. He looked old, worn out, and feeble. But she assumed he was none of those things. A name was called, the person allowed to step forward. A youngish man spoke for the prisoner, a few words were exchanged, and it was over. Darlene's case was the fifth called. When her name was uttered, she snapped to attention and the guard pushed her forward. The charge was read, and she was asked how she would plead.

"Not guilty, Your Honor." Hildon then asked about bail. He stated that she had turned herself in, was a mother of two young children, and wasn't likely to flee. The prosecutor requested that no bail be given. The judge stroked his chin, staring at Darlene for what seemed like minutes. Finally, he spoke.

"Bail is set at $500,000 dollars." He banged his gavel. The guard stepped forward, grabbed Darlene's shoulder and pulled her back. He was intent on re-cuffing her when Hildon interrupted him.

"Let her go. Bail is being paid as I speak." Darlene looked at him gratefully. She stepped out and followed him from the courtroom. He escorted her to the offices where she was handed papers to sign and other papers that outlined the conditions of her release.

"C'mon, I'll either drive you home or take you to breakfast.

Which is it?"

"I've had something to eat. I'd like to go home. Do you know when the trial is?"

"Not yet, but it'll be at least a year before it happens. He patted her on the arm.

"You be good and don't do anything stupid. I'll keep in touch. Mike wants me to handle the trial. I'll have to go over things with you from time to time. Here's my card."

He dropped her off, watched her go in and then left. Mike was at work but Dolly was there. The girls were at school and her father was asleep. She gratefully accepted a cup of coffee and sat silently in her kitchen looking around, unable to believe that she was actually there. She put the emptied coffee cup down and taking the phone, tried to track down her husband. When she found him, she exulted, "Hi, darling…I'm home."

"You got bail?"

"Yes. I'm in the kitchen. Oh Mike I can't believe I'm actually in my own kitchen."

"I'll drop in after lunch. I made superintendent, so I'm not on the road so much. If it's quiet, I can take time off during the day. I'll be by about two for a bit." She hung up and went upstairs. First, she looked into her and Mike's room, then she checked the children's rooms. Everything was strange to her. It was like she'd been away for years instead of nine months. She threw herself down on the bed and tried hard to relax. It didn't work. And she lay as if in the middle of a dream that hadn't yet ended.

When Darlene arose, Mike was in the kitchen. She hurried downstairs, and he handed her a cup of coffee.

"Have a good sleep?"

"No. I'm so worried about everything. Mike… I'm scared.

"Just take each day as it comes. You'll have to try and relax. You're not going to take on work, baby, just be a mother. The girls need you. Dolly has been carrying a heavy load and you're going to take it off her. I'm putting my foot down.

While she and Mike were talking, Darlene was searching through drawers. First she opened drawers in the kitchen and then moved to the living room. Mike followed. As she pulled open the drawer of a small cabinet, he snapped at her "What are you looking for? As if I didn't know."

"Where are the guns we used to keep around?"

"They are all locked up. I don't want to see you with a gun around here. One of your bail conditions is that you have nothing to do with firearms. I ordered that condition myself. You're finished with guns."

"How do I protect myself?"

"The same way the woman next door protects herself. You call for help. I'm not on the road any more and therefore not in the danger I used to be in. It's safe now, and you don't need to go around armed. Case closed."

"I'm glad that you're taking care of me. Can I take the girls shopping?"

"Anytime. You're not in danger any more."

"Oh Mike I'm so glad to be home."

One morning, early, there was a knock on the door and Mike went to answer it. She heard his exclamation and came to the door also. A man stood there. She gasped. Mike didn't know this man, but she did.

"Fredrick…is that you? What are you doing here? I can't believe my eyes. Mike…this is my oldest brother. He's three years younger than me. Fredrick, c'mon in and start answering questions. She led the way to the kitchen where they were having breakfast. So far, Fredrick hadn't said a word.

"Look girls…here's your uncle Fredrick from Russia. You're not here to bring me trouble, are you? She looked at her brother meaningfully. Finally, he spoke.

"I'm not only not bringing you trouble, I'm here to help you. I spotted a file in Russia and I removed it. Then I destroyed it and all copies of it. There is no record of you ever being in Russia, there is no record of you leaving Russia, no records at all. For this I want your help. He blurted it out fast, as if he had it memorized. Then he waited, with a look of helplessness on his face.

"What kind of help?"

"I want to escape from Russia, come to America and hide until I can get citizenship. I don't want to be in the army… I can't stand it. I need your help."

"What about Peter?"

"He's in Switzerland, hiding also. They conscripted him, but he fled. He has someone taking care of him. He will come here also but not now. I helped you and now you must help me."

"How can I help you? I'm facing a murder charge. I have no power."

"First, I need a place to stay. I'm at the Palmer House but I can't stay there indefinitely. Second, darling sister, I need a sponsor to allow me to remain in this country. I've checked, and I can remain here if you'll sponsor me."

"You can stay here…can't he, Mike? Do I have to sign papers?"

"Sure he can stay here for a while. The rules are strict around here right now though. We have a room you can use. What forms does she have to sign and do you have them with you?"

"I have the forms." He dug into the shiny black briefcase he was carrying and pulled out a sheaf of papers.

"I don't think it will cause anybody trouble. If she doesn't want to sign Mike, perhaps you could. Your signature would carry more weight."

"I'll sign if I'm allowed to. We don't want to draw attention to my wife right now. Welcome to America, brother!" He reached out to shake hands and instead, pulled Fredrick to him in a bear hug. Darlene smiled and smiled.

ABOUT THE AUTHOR

Gordon Marx was born in a small town in central British Columbia. For health reasons (asthma) he ran away from home at the age of 14 and supported himself from then on. At age 21 he traveled to Australia where he stayed 4 years, working at everything from a sheep station to working on the railroad with jobs as bartender in between.

He wasn't fully aware of his abilities until he returned to Canada and met a woman who became his friend. She recognised that he had a good mind and an unusually good memory so, she recommended that he attend college. This was an intimidating step for a person with only grade 8 but he followed her advice and studied English. The rest is history.

More about *Darlene Milanovich* and author Gordon Marx can be found at **darlenemilanovich.com.** If you would like to order copies of this book, please contact the author at **darlenemilanovich.com.**

CPSIA information can be obtained
at www.ICGtesting.com
Printed in the USA
LVOW11s0829061216
516009LV00001B/3/P

9 781460 289846